Uncles Josh's Punkin Centre Stories

Cal Stewart

Contents

UNCLES JOSH'S PUNKIN CENTRE STORIES

BY

Cal Stewart

Preface

To the Reader.

The one particular object in writing this book is to furnish you with an occasional laugh, and the writer with an occasional dollar. If you get the laugh you have your equivalent, and the writer has his.

In Uncle Josh Weathersby you have a purely imaginary character, yet one true to life. A character chuck full of sunshine and rural simplicity. Take him as you find him, and in his experiences you will observe there is a bright side to everything.

Sincerely Yours

Cal Stewart

Life Sketch of Author

THE author was born in Virginia, on a little patch of land, so poor we had to fertilize it to make brick. Our family, while having cast their fortunes with the South, was not a family ruined by the war; we did not have anything when the war commenced, and so we held our own. I secured a common school education, and at the age of twelve I left home, or rather home left me--things just petered out. I was slush cook on an Ohio River Packet; check clerk in a stave and heading camp in the knobs of Tennessee, Virginia and Georgia; I helped lay the track of the M. K. & T. R. R., and was chambermaid in a livery stable. Made my first appearance on the stage at the National Theatre in Cincinnati, Ohio, and have since then chopped cord wood, worked in a coal mine, made cross ties (and walked them), worked on a farm, taught a district school (made love to the big girls), run a threshing machine, cut bands, fed the machine and ran the engine. Have been a freight and passenger brakeman, fired and ran a locomotive; also a freight train conductor and check clerk in a freight house; worked on the section; have been a shot gun messenger for the Wells, Fargo Company. Have been with a circus, minstrels, farce comedy, burlesque and dramatic productions; have been with good shows, bad shows, medicine shows, and worse, and some shows where we had landlords singing in the chorus. Have played variety houses and vaudeville houses; have slept in a box car one night, and a swell hotel the next; have been a traveling salesman (could spin as many yarns as any of them). For the past four years have made the Uncle Josh stories for the talking machine. The Lord only knows what next!

My Old Yaller Almanac

Hangin' on the
Kitchen Wall

I'M sort of fond of readin' one
thing and another,

So I've read promiscus like
whatever cum my way,

And many a friendly argument's cum up 'tween
me and mother,

'Bout things that I'd be readin' settin' round
a rainy day.

Sometimes it jist seemed to me thar wa'nt
no end of books,

Some made fer useful readin' and some jist
made fer looks;

But of all the different books I've read,
thar's none comes up at all

To My Old Yaller Almanac, Hangin' on
the Kitchen Wall.

I've always liked amusement, of the good
and wholesome kind,

It's better than a doctor, and it elevates the
mind;

So, often of an evening, when the farm
chores all were done,

I'd join the games the boys would play, gosh
how I liked the fun;

And once thar wuz a minstrel troop, they
showed at our Town Hall,

A jolly lot of fellers, 'bout twenty of 'em all.

Wall I went down to see 'em, but their
jokes, I knowed 'em all,

Read 'em in My Old Yaller Almanac,
Hangin' on the Kitchen Wall.

Thar wuz Ezra Hoskins, Deacon Brown and
a lot of us old codgers,

Used to meet down at the grocery store,
what wuz kept by Jason Rogers.

There we'd set and argufy most every market
day,

Chawin' tobacker and whittlin' sticks to pass
the time away;

And many a knotty problem has put us on
our mettle,

Which we felt it wuz our duty to duly solve
and settle;

Then after they had said their say, who
thought they knowed it all,

I'd floor 'em with some facts I'd got

From My Old Yaller Almanac, Hangin' on
the Kitchen Wall.

It beats a regular cyclopedium, that old
fashioned yeller book,

And many a pleasant hour in readin' it I've
took;

Somehow I've never tired of lookin' through
its pages,

Seein' of the different things that's happened
in all ages.

One time I wuz elected a Justice of the
Peace,

To make out legal documents, a mortgage
or a lease,

Them tricks that lawyers have, you bet I
knowed them all,

Learned them in My Old Yaller Almanac,
Hangin' on the Kitchen Wall.

So now I've bin to New York, and all your
sights I've seen,

I s'pose that to you city folks I must look
most awful green,

Gee whiz, what lots of fun I've had as I
walked round the town,

Havin' Bunco Steerers ask me if I wasn't
Mr. Hiram Brown.

I've rode on all your trolloly cars, and hung
onto the straps,

When we flew around the corners, sat on
other peoples' laps,

Hav'nt had no trouble, not a bit at all,

Read about your city in My Old Yaller
Almanac, Hangin' on the Kitchen Wall.

Uncle Josh Weathersby's Arrival in New York

WALL, fer a long time I had my mind made up that I'd cum down to New York, and so a short time ago, as I had my crops all gathered in and produce sold I calculated as how it would be a good time to come down here. Folks at home said I'd be buncoed or have my pockets picked fore I'd bin here mor'n half an hour; wall, I fooled 'em a little bit, I wuz here three days afore they buncoed me. I spose as how there are a good many of them thar bunco fellers around New York, but I tell you them thar street keer conductors take mighty good care on you. I wuz ridin' along in one of them keers, had my pockit book right in my hand, I alowed no feller would pick my pockits and git it long as I had it in my hand, and it shet up tight as a barrel when the cider's workin'. Wall that conductor feller he jest kept his eye on me, and every little bit he'd put his head in the door and say "hold fast." But I'm transgressin' from what I started to tell ye. I wuz ridin' along in one of them sleepin' keers comin' here, and along in the night some time I felt a feller rummagin' around under my bed, and I looked out jest in time to see him goin' away with my boots, wall I knowed the way that train wuz a runnin' he couldn't git off with them without breakin' his durned neck, but in about half an hour he brot them back, guess they didn't fit him. Wall I wuz sort of glad he took em cause he hed em all shined up slicker 'n a new tin whistle. Wall when I got up in the mornin' my trubbles commenced. I wuz so crouded up like, durned if I could git my clothes on, and when I did git em on durned if my pants wa'nt on hind side afore, and my socks got all tangled up in that little fish net along side of the bed and I couldn't git em out, and I lost a bran new collar button that I traded Si Pettingill a huskin' peg fer, and I got my right boot on my left foot and the left one on the right foot, and I wuz so durned badly mixed up I didn't know which way the train wuz a runnin', and I bumped my head on the roof of the bed over me, and then sot down right suddin like to think it over when some feller cum along and stepped right squar on my bunion and I let out a war whoop you could a heerd over in the next county. Wall, along cum that durned porter and told me I wuz a wakin' up everybody in the keer. Then I started in to hunt fer my collar button, cause I sot a right smart store by that button, thar warns another one like it in Punkin Centre, and I thought it would be kind of doubtful if they'd have any like it in New York, wall I see one stuck right in the wall so I tried to git it out with my jack knife, when along came that durned black jumpin' jack dressed in soldier clothes and ast me what I wanted, and I told him I didn't want anything perticler, then he told me to quit ringin' the bell, guess he wuz a little crazy, I didn't see no bell. Wall, finally I got my clothes on and went into a room whar they had a row of little troughs to wash in, and fast as I could pump water in the durned thing it run out of a little hole in the bottom of the trough so I jest had to grab a handful and then pump some more. Wall after that things went along purty well fer a right smart while, then I et a snack out of my carpet bag and felt purty good. Wall that train got to runnin' slower and slower 'till it stopped at every house and when it cum to a double house it stopped twice. I hed my ticket in my hat and I put my head out of the window to look at suthin' when the wind blew my hat off and I lost the durned old ticket, wall the conductor made me buy another one. I hed to buy two tickets to ride once, but I fooled him, he don't know a durned thing about it and when he finds it out he's goin to be the maddest conductor on that railroad, I got a round trip ticket and I ain't a goin' back on his durned old road. When I got off the ferry boat down here I commenced to think I wuz about the best lookin' old feller what ever cum to New York, thar wuz a lot of fellers down thar with buggies and kerridges and one thing and another, and jest the minnit they seen me they all

commenced to holler--handsome--handsome. I didn't know I wuz so durned
good lookin'. One feller tried to git my carpet bag and another tried
to git my umbreller, and I jest told 'em to stand back or durned if I
wouldn't take a wrestle out of one or two of them, then I asked one of
'em if he could haul me up to the Sturtevessant hotel, and by gosh I
never heered a feller stutter like that feller did in all my life,
he said ye-ye-ye-yes sir, and I said wall how much air you a goin' to
charge me, and he said f-f-f-fif-fif-fifty c-c-cents, and I sed wall I
guess I'll ride with you, but don't stop to talk about it any more cause
I'd kinder like to git thar. Wall we started out and when we stopped we
wuz away up at the other end of the town whar thar warn't many houses,
and I sed to him, this here ain't the Sturtevessant hotel, and he sed
n-n-n-no n-s-s-n-no sir, I sed why didn't you let me out at the
hotel like I told ye, and he sed, b-b-b-be c-c-c b-b-be cause I
c-c-c-c-couldn't s-s-s-say w-w-w-whoa q-q-q-q-quick enough. Wall I hed a
great time with that feller, but I got here at last.

Uncle Josh in Society

WALL, I did'nt suppose when I cum down here to New York that I wuz a goin to flop right into the middle of high toned society, but I guess that's jist about what I done. You see I had an old friend a livin' down here named Henry Higgins, and I wanted to see Henry mighty bad. Henry and me, we wuz boys together down home at Punkin Centre, and I hadn't seen him in a long time. Wall, I got a feller to look up his name in the city almanac, and he showed me whar Henry lived, away up on a street called avenue five. Wall when I seen Henry's house it jist about took my breath away, I wuz that clar sot back. Henry's house is a good deal bigger'n the court house at Punkin Centre. Wall at first I didn't know whether to go in or not, but finally I mustered up my courage, and I went up and rang some new fangled door bell, when a feller with knee britches on cum out and wanted to know who it wuz I wanted to see. Gosh I couldn't say anything fer about a minnit, that feller jist looked to me like a picter I'd seen in a story book. Wall finally I told him I wanted to see Henry Higgins, if it wuz the same Henry I used to know down home at Punkin Centre. Wall I guess Henry he must a heered me talkin', cause he jist cum out and grabbed me by both hands and sed, "why Josh Weathersby, how do you do, cum right in." Wall he took me into the house and introduced me to more wimmin folks than I ever seen before in all my life at one time. I guess they were havin' some kind of society doins at Henry's house, one old lady sed to me, "my dear Mr. Weathersby, I am so pleased to meet you, I've heered Mr. Higgins speak about you so often." Wall by chowder, I got to blushin' so it cum pretty near settin' my hair on fire, but I sed, wall now I'm right glad to know you, you kind-er put me in mind of old Nancy Smith down hum, and Nancy, she's bin tryin' to git married past forty seasons that I kin remember on. Wall Henry took me off into a room by myself, and when I got on my store clothes and my new calf skin boots, I tell you I looked about as scrimptious as any of them. Wall they had a dance, I think they called it a cowtillion, and that wuz whar I wuz right to hum, I jist hopped out on the floor, balanced to partners, swung on the corners, and cut up more capers than any young feller thar, it jist looked as if all the ladies wanted to dance with me. One lady wanted to know if I danced the german, but I told her I only danced in English.

Wall after that we had something to eat in the dinin' room, and I hadn't any more'n got sot down and got to eatin right good, when that durn fool with the knee britches on insulted me, he handed me a little wash bowl with a towel round it, and I told him he needn't cast any insinuations at me, cause I washed my hands afore I cum in. If it hadn't a bin in Henry's house I'd took a wrestle out of him. Wall they had a lot of furrin dishes, sumthin what they called beef all over mud, and another what they called a-charlotte russia-a little shavin' mug made out of cake and full of sweetened lather, wall that was mighty good eatin', though it took a lot of them, they wasn't very fillin'. Then they handed me somethin' what they called ice cream, looked to me like a hunk of casteel soap, wall I stuck my fork in it and tried to bite it, and it slipped off and got inside my vest, and in less than a minnit I wuz froze from my chin to my toes. I guess I cut a caper at Henry's house.

Uncle Josh in a Chinese Laundry

I S'POSE I got tangled up the other day with the dogondest lookin'
critter I calculate I ever seen in all my born days, and I've bin around
purty considerable. I'd seen all sorts of cooriosoties and monstrosities
in cirkuses and meenagerys, but that wuz the fust time I'd ever seen
a critter with his head and tail on the same end. You see I sed to a
feller, now whar abouts in New York do you folks git your washin' done;
when I left hum to come down here I lowed I had enuff with me to do
me, but I've stayed here a little longer than I calculated to, and if I
don't git some washin' done purty soon, I'll have to go and jump in the
river.
Wall he wuz a bligin sort of a feller, and he told me thar wuz a place
round the corner whar a feller done all the washin', so I went round,
and there was a sine on the winder what sed Hop Quick, or Hop Soon, or
jump up and hop, or some other kind of a durned hop; and then thar wuz
a lot of figers on the winder that I couldn't make head nor tail on; it
jist looked to me like a chicken with mud on its feet had walked over
that winder.

Wall I went in to see bout gittin' my washin' done, and gosh all spruce
gum, thar was one of them pig tailed heathen Chineeze, he jist looked
fer all the world like a picter on Aunt Nancy Smith's tea cups. I wuz
sort of sot back fer a minnit, coz 'I sed to myself--I don't spose this
durned critter can talk English; but seein' as how I'm in here, I might
as well find out. So I told him I'd like to git him to do some washin'
fer me, and he commenced a talkin' some outlandish lingo, sounded to me

like cider runnin' out of a jug, somethin' like--ung tong oowong fang kai moi oo ung we, velly good washee. Wall I understood the last of it and jist took his word fer the rest, so I giv him my clothes and he giv me a little yeller ticket that he painted with a brush what he had, and I'll jist bet a yoke of steers agin the holler in a log, that no livin' mortal man could read that ticket; it looked like a fly had fell into the ink bottle and then crawled over the paper. Wall I showed it to a gentleman what was a standin' thar when I cum out, and I sed to him--mister, what in thunder is this here thing, and he sed "Wall sir that's a sort of a lotery ticket; every time you leave your clothes thar to have them washed you git one of them tickets, and then you have a chance to draw a prize of some kind." So I sed--wall now I want to know, how much is the blamed thing wuth, and he sed "I spose bout ten cents," and I told him if he wanted my chants for ten cents he could hav it, I didn't want to get tangled up in any lotery gamblin' bizness with that saucer faced scamp. So he giv me ten cents and he took the ticket, and in a couple of days I went round to git my washin', and that pig tailed heathen he wouldn't let me hev em, coz I'd lost that lotery ticket. So I sed--now look here Mr. Hop Soon, if you don't hop round and git me my collars and ciffs and other clothes what I left here, I'll be durned if I don't flop you in about a minnit, I will by chowder. Wall that critter he commenced hoppin around and a talkin faster 'n a buzz saw could turn, and all I could make out wuz--mee song lay tang moo me oo lay ung yong wo say mee tickee. Wall I seen jist as plain as could be that he wuz a tryin' to swindle me outen my clothes, so I made a grab fer him, and in less 'n a minnit we wuz a rollin' round on the floor; fust I wuz on top, and then Mr. Hop Soon wuz on top, and you couldn't hav told which one of us the pig tail belonged to. We upset the stove and kicked out the winder, and I sot Mr. Hop Soon in the wash tub, and when I got out of thar I had somebody's washin' in one hand and about five yards of that pig tail in tother, and Mr. Hop Soon, he wuz standin' thar yellin'--ung wa moo ye song ki le yung noy song oowe pelecee, pelecee, pelecee. I had quite a time with that heathen critter.

Uncle Josh in a Museum

WHEN I wuz in New York one day I wuz a walkin' along down the street
when I cum to a theater or play doins' of some kind or other, so I got
to lookin' at the picters, and I noticed whar it sed it only cost ten
cents to go in, and I alowed I might as well go in and see it. Wall I
don't spose I'd bin in thar over five minutes afore I made myself the
laffin' stock of every one in thar. I noticed a feller a sottin' thar
gittin' his boots blacked, and thar was a durned little pick pockit a
pickin' his pockits. Wall I didn't want to see him git robbed, so I went
right up to him and I sed--look out mister, you air gittin' your pockits
picked, wall sir, that durned cuss never sed a word and every body
commenced to laff, and I looked round to see what they wuz a laffin'
at, and it wan't no man at all, nothin' only a durned old wax figger.
I never felt so durned foolish since the day I popped the question to
Samantha. Wall then I looked round a spell longer, and thar wuz a feller
what they called the human pin cushion, and he wuz stuck chock full of
needles and pins and looked like a hedge hog; he'd be a mighty handy
feller at a quiltin'. Wall, then a feller cum along and sed, "everybody
over to this end of the hall." Wall, I went along with the rest of them,
and durn my buttins if thar wa'nt a feller what had more picters painted
on him than thar is in a story book. Wall, I'd jist got to lookin' at
him when that feller what had charge sed, "right this way everybody,"
and we all went into whar they wuz havin' the theater doins', and I got
sot down and a feller cum out and sung a song I hadn't heered since I
wuz a youngster. Neer as I kin remember it wuz this way--

Kind friends I hadn't had but one sleigh ride this year,
　　And I cum within one of not bein' here,
The facts I'll relate near as I kin remember,
　　It happened some time 'bout last December.
　　　　Li too ra loo ri too ra loo
　　　　　ri too ra loo la ri do.

The load was composed of both girls and boys,
　　All tryin' to outdo the other in noise.
And the way that we guarded agin the cold weather
　　Wuz settin' all up spoon fashion together.
　　　　Li too ra loo ri too ra loo
　　　　　ri too ra loo ri li do.

Wall, they had a parrit in that place and the way he sputtered and jabbered and talked! He wuz a whole show all to himself. Wall, I bought one of them birds from a feller one time--he said it wuz a good talker. Wall, I took it hum and hed it about three months, and it never sed a durned word. I put in most of my spare time tryin' to git it to say "Uncle Josh," but the durned critter wouldn't do it, so I got mad at him one day and throwed him out in the barn yard amongst the chickens, and left him thar. Wall, when I went out the next mornin', I tell you thar wuz a sight. Half of them chickens wuz dead, and the rest of 'em wuz skeered to death, and that durned parrit had a rooster by the neck up agin the barn, and jist a givin' him an awful whippin', and every time he'd hit him he'd say, "Now you say Uncle Josh, gol durn you, you say Uncle Josh."

Uncle Josh in Wall Street

I USED to read in our town paper down home at Punkin Centre a whole lot
about Wall street and them bulls and bears, and one thing and another,
so I jist sed to myself--now Joshua, when you git down to New York City,
that's jist what you want to see. Wall, when I got to New York, I got
a feller to show me whar it wuz, and I'll be durned if I know why they
call it Wall street; it didn't hav any wall round it. I walked up and
down it bout an hour and a half, and I couldn't find any stock exchange
or see any place fer watterin' any stock. I couldn't see a pig nor a
cow, nor a sheep nor a calf, or anything else that looked like stock
to me. So finally I sed to a gentleman--Mister, whar do they keep the
menagery down here. He sed "what menagery?" I sed the place whar they've
got all them bulls and bears a fitin'. Wall he looked at me as though he
thought I wuz crazy, and I guess he did, but he sed "you cum along with
me, guess I can show you what you want to see." Wall I went along with
him, and he took me up to some public institushun, near as I could make
out it wuz a loonytick asylem. Wall he took me into a room about two
akers and a half squar, and thar wuz about two thousand of the crazyest
men in thar I ever seen in all my life. The minnit I sot eyes on them I
knowed they wuz all crazy, and I'd hav to umer them if I got out of thar
alive. One feller wuz a standin' on the top of a table with a lot of
papers in his hand, and a yellin' like a Comanche injin, and all the
rest of them wuz tryin' to git at him. Finally I sed to one of
'em--Mister, what are you a tryin' to do with that feller up thar on the
table? And he sed, "Wall he's got five thousand bushels of wheat and we
are tryin' to git it away from him." Wall, jist the minnit he sed that I

knowed fer certain they wuz all crazy, cos nobody but a crazy man would ever think he had five thousand bushels of wheat in his coat and pants pockits. Wall when they wan't a looking I got out of thar, and I felt mighty thankful to git out. There wuz a feller standin' on the front steps; he had a sort of a unyform on; I guess he wuz Superintendent of the institushun; he talked purty sassy to me. I sed, Mister, what time does the fust car go up town. He sed "the fust one went about twenty-five years ago." I sed to him--is that my car over thar? He sed "no sir, that car belongs to the street car company." I sez, wall guess I'll take it anyhow. He says "you'd better not, thar's bin a good many cars missed around here lately." I sed, wall now, I want to know, is thar anything round here any fresher than you be? He sed, "yes, sir, that bench you're a sotten on is a little fresher; they painted it about ten minnits ago." Wall, I got up and looked, and durned if he wasn't right.

Uncle Josh and the Fire Department

ONE day in New York, I thot I'd rite a letter home. Wall after I'd got
it all writ, I sed to the landlord of the tavern--now, whar abouts in
New York do you keep the post offis? And he sed, "what do you want with
the post offis?" So I told him I'd jist writ a letter home to mother and
Samantha Ann, and I'd like to go to the post offis and mail it. And he
told me "you don't have to go to the post offis, do you see that little
box on the post thar on the corner?" I alowed as how I did. Wall he
says, "You jist go out thar and put your letter in that box, and it
will go right to the post offis." I sed--wall now, gee whiz, ain't that
handy. Wall I went out thar, and I had a good deal of trouble in gittin'
the box open, and when I did git it open, thar wan't any place to put
my letter, thar wuz a lot of notes and hooks and hinges, and a lot
of readin,' it sed--"pull on the hook twice and turn the knob," or
somethin, like that, I couldn't jist rightly make it out. Wall I yanked
on that hook 'till I tho't I'd pull it out by the roots, but I couldn't
git the durned thing open, then I turned on the knob two or three times,
and that didn't do any good, so I pulled on the hook and turned on the
knob at the same time, and jist then I think all the fire bells in New
York commenced to ringin' all to onct. Wall I looked round to see whar
the fire wuz, and a lot of fire ingines and hook and ladder wagons cum
a gallopin' up to whar I stood, and they had a big sody water bottle on
wheels, and it busted and squirted sody water all over me. Wall one of
them fire fellers, lookin' jist like I'd seen them in picters in Ezra
Hoskin's insurance papers, he cum up to me madder'n a hornet, and he sed
"what are you tryin' to do with that box?" So I told him I'd jist writ

a letter home, and I wuz a tryin' to mail it. He sed "why you durned
old green horn, you've called out the hull fire department of New York
City." Wall I guess you could have knocked me down with a feather. I
sed--wall you'r a purty healthy lookin' lot of fellers, it won't hurt
ye any to go back, will it? Wall he sed, "thars your letter box over on
thother corner, now you let this box alone." Wall they all drove away,
and I went over to the other box, but I didn't know whether to touch it
or not, I didn't know but maybe I'd call out the state legislater if
I opened it. Wall while I wuz a standin' thar a feller cum along and
looked all round, and when he thot thar wan't any body watchin' him, he
opened that box and commenced takin' the letters out. Wall I'd heered
a whole lot 'bout them post offis robbers, when I wuz post master down
home at Punkin Center, so jist arrested him right thar, I took him by
the nap of the neck and flopped him right down on the side walk, and sot
on him, I hollered--MURDER! PERLEES! and every other thing I could think
of, and a lot of constables and town marshalls cum a runnin' up, and
one of them sed "what are you holdin' this man fer?" and I told him I'd
caught him right in the act of robbin' the United States Post Offis, and
by gosh I arrested him. Wall they all commenced a laffin', and I found
out I'd arrested one of the post masters of New York City.

I lost mother's letter and she never did git it.

Uncle Josh in an Auction Room

I'D seen a good many funny things in New York at one time and another, so the last day I wuz thar, I wuz a packin' up my traps, a gittin' ready to go home, when I jist conclooded I'd go out and buy somethin' to remember New York by.

Wall I wuz a walkin' along down the street when I cum to a place whar they wuz auckshuneerin' off a lot of things. I stopped to see what they had to sell. Wall that place wuz jist chuck full of old-fashioned cooriositys. I saw an old book thar, they sed it wuz five hundred years old, and it belonged at one time to Loois the Seventeenth or Eighteenth, or some of them old rascals; durned if I believe anybody could read it.

Wall I commenced a biddin' on different things, but it jist looked as though everybody had more money than I did, and they sort of out-bid me; but finally they put up an old-fashioned shugar bowl fer sale, and I wanted to git that mighty bad, cos I thought as how mother would like it fust rate. Wall I commenced a biddin' on it, and it wuz knocked down to me fer three dollars and fifty cents I put my hand in my pockit to git my pockit book to pay fer it, and by gosh it was gone. So I went up to the feller what wuz a sellin' the things, and I sed--now look here mister, will you jist wait a minnit with your "goin' at thirty make it thirty-five, once, twice, three times a goin'", and he sed "wall now what's the matter with you?" And I sed, there's matter enuff, by gosh; when I cum in here I had a pockit book in my pockit, had fifty dollars in it, and I lost it somewhars round here; I wish you'd say to the feller what found it that I'll give five dollars fer it; another feller sed "make it ten," another sed "give you twenty," and another sed "go you twenty-five."

Durned if I know which one of 'em got it; when I left they wuz still a biddin' on it.

Advice--Advice is somethin' the other feller can't use, so he gives it to you.--Punkin Centre Philosophy.

Uncle Josh on a Fifth Ave. 'Bus

I WUZ always sort of fond of ridin', so I guess while I wuz down in New York I rode on about everything they've got to ride on thar. I wuz on hoss cars and hot air cars, and them sky light elevated roads. Wall, I had jist about cum to the conclushun that every street in New York had a different kind of a street car on it, but I found one that didn't have care of any kind, I think they call it Avenoo Five. Wall, I wuz a standin' thar one day a watchin' the people and things go by, when all to onct along cum the durndest lookin' contraption I calculate I ever seen in my life. It wuz a sort of a wagon, kind of a cross between a band wagon and a hay rack, and it had a pair of stairs what commenced at the hind end and rambled around all over the wagon. I sed to a gentleman standin' thar: "Mr. in the name of all that's good and bad, what do you call that thing?" He sed: "Wall, sir, that's a Fifth Avenoo 'bus." I sed: "Wall, now, I want to know, kin I ride on it?" And he sed: "You kin if you've got a nickel." Wall, I got in and sot down, and I jist about busted my buttins a laffin' at things what happened in that 'bus. Thar wuz a young lady cum in and sot down, and she had a little valise in her hand, 'bout a foot squar. Wall, she opened the valise and took out a purse and shet the valise, then she opened the purse and took out a dime, and shet the purse, opened the valise and put in the purse, and shet the valise, then she handed the dime to a feller sottin' out on the front of the 'bus, and he give her a nickel back. Then she opened the valise and took out the purse, shet the valise and opened the purse and put in the nickel and shet the purse, opened the valise and put in the purse and shet the valise, then sed, "Stop the bus, please." Wall, I had to snicker right out, though I done my best not to, but I jist couldn't help it. I didn't have any small change so I handed the feller a five-dollar bill. Wall, that feller jist sot and looked at it fer a spell, then he sed "whoa!" stopped the hosses, cum round to the hind end of the 'bus and he sed: "Who give me that five-dollar bill?" I sed: "I did, and it was a good one, too." He sed: "Wall, you cum out here, I want to see you." Wall, I didn't know what he wanted, but I jist made up my mind if he indulged in any foolishness with me I'd flop him in about a minnit. Wall, I got out thar, and he sed: "Now look here, honest injun, did you give me that five-dollar bill?" I sed: "Yes, sir, that's jist what I done," and he sed, "Wall, now, which one of the hosses do you want?" Gosh, I don't believe I'd gin him five dollars fer the whole durned outfit.

Ambition--Somethin' that has made one man a senator, and another man a convict.--Punkin Centre Philosophy

Uncle Josh in a Department Store

ONE day while I wuz in New York I sed to a feller, now whar kin I find
one of them stores whar they hav purty near everything to sell what
thar is on earth, and he sed "I guess you mean a department store, don't
you?" I sed, wall I don't know bout that; they may sell departments
at one of them stores, but what I want to git is some muzlin and some
caliker. Wall he showed me which way to go, and I started out, and
wuz walkin' along down the street lookin' at things, when some feller
throwed a bananer peelin' on the sidewalk. Wall now I don't think much
of a man what throws a bananer peelin' on the sidewalk, and I don't
think much of a bananer what throws a man on the sidewalk, neether.
Wall, by chowder, my foot hit that bananer peelin' and I went up in the
air, and cum down ker-plunk, and fer about a minnit I seen all the stars
what stronomy tells about, and some that haint been discovered yit.
Wall jist as I wuz pickin' myself up a little boy cum runnin' 'cross the
street and he sed "Oh mister, won't you please do that agin, my mother
didn't see you do it." Wall I wish I could a got my hands on that little
rascal fer about a minnit, and his mother would a seen me do it.

I found one of them stores finally, and I got on the inside and told a
feller what I wanted, and he sent me over to a red-headed girl, and she
sent me over to a bald-headed feller; she sed he didn't have anythin' to
do only walk the floor and answer questions. Wall I went up to him and I
sed, mister I'm sort of a stranger round here, wish you'd show me round
'til I do a little bargainin'. And he sed "Oh you git out, you've got
hay seed in your hair." Wall I jist looked at that bald head of hisn,

and I sed, wall now, you haint got any hay seed in YOUR hair, hav you?
Everybody commenced a laffin', and he got purty riled, so he sed, smart
like, "jist step this way, please." Wall he showed me round and I bought
what I wanted, and when I cum to pay the feller what I had to pay,
it didn't look as though I wuz a goin' to git any of my money back. I
handed him a ten dollar bill, and he jist took it and put it in a
little baskit and hitched it onto a wire, and the durned thing commenced
runnin' all over the store. Wall now you can jist bet your boots I
lit out right after it; I chased it up one side and down the other, I
knocked down five or six wimmin clerks, and I upset five or six bargain
counters; I took a wrastle out of that bald-headed feller, and jist
then some one commenced to holler "CASH" and I sed yep, that's what I'm
after. Wall I chased that durned little baskit round 'til I got up to
it, and when I did I was right thar whar I started from. Gee whiz, I
never felt more foolish in all my life.

Prosperity--Consists principally of contentment; for the man
who is contented is prosperous, in his own way of thinking,
though his neighbors may have a different opinion.
--Punkin Centre Philosophy.

Uncle Josh's Comments on the Signs Seen in New York

I SEEN a good many funny things when I wuz in New York, but I think some
of the sines what they've got on some of the bildins' are 'bout as funny
as anything I ever seen in my life.

I wuz walkin' down the street one day and I seen a sine, it sed "Quick
Lunch." Wall, I felt a little hungry, so I went into the resturant or
bordin' house, or whatever they call it, and they had some sines hangin'
on the walls in thar that jist about made me laff all over. I noticed
one sine sed "Put your trust in the Lord," and right under it wuz
another sine what sed "Try our mince pies." Wall, I tried one of them,
and I want to tell you right now, if you eat many of them mince pies you
want to put your trust in the Lord.

Wall, I got out of thar, and I walked along fer quite a spell, and
finally I cum to a store what had a lot of red, white and blue, and
yeller and purple lights in the winder. Wall, I stopped to look at it,
cos it wuz a purty thing, and they had a sine in that winder that jist
tickled me, it sed, "Frog in your throat 10C." I wouldn't put one of
them critters in my throat fer ten dollars.

Wall, jist a little further up the street I seen another sine what
sed "Boots blacked on the inside." Now, any feller what gits his boots
blacked on the inside ain't got much respect fer his socks. I git mine
blacked on the outside. Then I cum to a sine what had a lot of 'lectric

lights shinin' on it, and I could read it jist as plain as day; so I happened to turn round and when I looked at that sine agin, it wa'nt the same sine at all, and jist then it changed right in front of my very eyes, and I cum to the conclooshun that some feller on the inside wuz a turnin' on it jist to have fun with folks, so I cum away; but I had a mighty good laff or two watchin' other folks git fooled, cos it would turn fust one way and then the t'other, and 'fore you could make up your mind what it wuz, the durned thing wouldn't be that at all.

A little further up the street I seen a sine what sed, "This is the door." Now, any durned fool could see it wuz a door. And then I seen another sine what sed "Walk in." Wall, now, I wunder how in thunder they thought a feller wuz a goin' to cum in, on hoss back, or on a bisickle, or how. And then I seen another sine, it wuz in a winder and had a lot of tools around it, and the sine sed, "Cast iron sinks." Wall, now, any durned fool what don't know that cast iron sinks, ought to have some one feel his head and find out what ails him.

Uncle Josh on a Street Car

NOW I'll jist bet I had more fun to the squar inch while I wuz in New York, than any old feller what ever broke out of a New England smoke house. I had a little the durnd'st time a ridin' on them street cars what they got thar. Wall I wa'nt a ridin' on 'emnear as much as I wuz a runnin' after 'em tryin' to ketch 'em. Gosh, I wuz a runnin' after street cars and fire ingines, and every durned thing with red wheels on it, I calculate I run about a mile and a half after a feller one day to tell him the water what he had in his wagon wuz all leakin' out, and when I caught up to him I found out it wuz a durned old sprinklin' cart.

Wall I got on one of them street cars one day, and it wuz purty crowded, and thar wa'nt any place fer me to sot down, so I had to hang onto one of them little harness straps along side of the car. So I got holt of a strap and I wuz hangin' on, when the conductor sed "old man, you'r goin' to be in the road thar, you'd better move up a little further, wall I moved up a little ways and I stepped on a feller's toe, and gee whiz, he got madder'n a wet hen, he sed, 'can't you see whar you'r a steppin'?" I sed, "guess I kin, but you brought them feet in here, and I've got to step some whar." Wall every one begin to laff, and the conductor sed, "old man you'r makin' too much trouble, you'll have to move for'ard again," and I got off 'n the gosh durned old car; I paid him a nickel to ride, but I guess I might as well have walked, I wuz a walkin' purty much all the time I wuz in thar.

Wall I got onto another car, and I got sot down, and I never laffed so

much in all my life. Up in one end of the car thar wuz a little slim
lady, and right along side of her wuz a big fleshy lady, and it didn't
look as though the little slim lady wuz a gittin' more'n about two cents
and a half worth of room, so finally she turned round to the fleshy lady
and sed, "they ought to charge by weight on this line," and the big lady
sed "Wall if they did they wouldn't stop fer you." Gosh I had to snicker
right out loud.

Thar wuz a little boy a sottin' alongside of the big lady, and three
ladys got onto the car all to onct, and thar wa'nt any place fer 'em to
sot down, and so the big lady sed--"little boy, you'd oughter git up
and let one of them ladys sot down," and the little boy sed, "you git up
and they can all sot down." Wall by that time your uncle wuz a laffin'
right out.

Sottin' right alongside of me wuz a lady and she had the purtiest little
baby I calculate I'd ever seen in all my born days, I wanted to be
sociable with the little feller so I jist sort of waved my hand at him,
and sed how-d'e-do baby, and that lady just looked et me scornful like
and sed "rubber," wall I wuz never more sot back, I guess you could
have knocked me down with a feather, I thought it was a genuine baby, I
didn't know the little thing was rubber.

Wall I noticed up in one end of the car thar wuz a little round masheen,
and the conductor had a clothes line tied to it, and every time he got
a nickel he'd yank on that clothes line, and fust it sed in and then it
sed out, I couldn't tell what all them little ins and outs meant, but I
jist cum to the conclusion it showed how much the conductor wuz in and
the company wuz out.

Wall I got to talkin' to that feller on the front end of the car, and he
wuz a purty nice sort of a feller, he showed me how every thing worked
and told me all about it, wall when I got off I sed--good bye, mister,

hope I'll see you agin some time, and he sed, "oh, I'll run across you one of these days," I told him by gosh he wouldn't run across me if I seen him a comin'.

My Fust Pair of Copper Toed Boots

THAR'S a feelin' of pleasure, mixed in with some pain,

That over my memory scoots,

When I think of my boyhood days once again

And my fust pair of copper toed boots.

How our folks stood around when I fust tried them on,

And bravely marched out on the floor,

And father remarked "thar a mighty good fit

And the best to be had at the store."

That night, I remember, I took them to bed,

With the rest of us little galoots,

And among other things in my prars which I sed

Wuz a reference to copper toed boots.

And then in the mornin' the fust one on hand

Wuz me and my new acquisition,

And thar wuzn't a spot in the house that I missed,

From the garret clar down to the kitchen.

Then with feelin's expandin', and huntin' fer room,

I concluded I'd help do the chores;

Fer I felt as though somethin' wuz goin' to bust

If I didn't git right out of doors.

But those boots they were new, and the ice it wuz slick,

And I couldn't get one way or tother,

And I jist had to stand right there in one spot

And holler like thunder fer mother.

But trouble's a blessing sometimes in disguise

Fer I larned right thar on the spot,

That the best sort of knowledge to hav in this world

Is that by experience taught.

So though many years have since passed away,

And I've ventured on various routes,

I'm still tryin' things jist as risky today

As my fust pair of copper toed boots.

Uncle Josh in Police Court

I NEVER wuz in a town in my life what had as many cort houses in it as New York has got. It jist seemed to me like every judge in New York had a cort house of his own, and most of them cort houses seemed to be along side of some markit house. Thar wuz the Jefferson Markit Cort, and the Essicks Markit Cort, and several other corts and markits, and markits and corts, I can't remember now. Wall, I used to be Jestice of the Peece down home at Punkin Center, and I wuz a little anxious to see how they handled law and jestice in New York City, so one mornin' I went down to one of them cort houses, and thar wuz more different kinds of people in thar than I ever seen afore. Thar wuz all kinds of nationalitys--Norweegans, Germans, Sweeds, Hebrews, and Skandynavians, Irish and colored folks, old and young, dirty and clean, good, bad and worse. The Judge, he wuz a sottin' up on the bench, and a sayin,: "Ten days; ten dollars; Geery society; foundlin' asylum; case dismissed; bring in the next prisoner," and the Lord only knows what else. Wall, some of the cases they tried in that cort house made me snicker right out loud. They brought in a little Irish feller, and the Judge sed: "Prisoner, what is your name?" And the little Irish feller sed: "Judge, your honor, my name is McGiness, Patrick McGiness." And the Judge sed: "Mr. McGiness, what is your occupation?" And the little Irish feller sed: "Judge, your honor, I am a sailor." The Judge sed: "Mr. McGiness, you don't look to me as though you ever saw a ship in all your life." And the little Irish feller sed: "Wall Judge, your honor, if I never saw a ship in me life, do you think I cum over from Ireland in a wagon?" The Judge sed: "Case dismissed. Bring in the next prisoner."

Wall, the next prisoner what they brought in had sort of an impediment in his talk, and the way he stuttered jist beat all. The Judge sed: "Prisoner, what is your name?" And the prisoner sed: "Jd-Jd-J-J-Judge, yr-yr-yo-yo-your h-h-h-hon-hon-honor, m-mm-my-my n-n-na-na-name is-is-is----." The Judge sed: "Never mind, that will do. Officer, what is this prisoner charged with?" And the officer sed: "Judge, your honor, the way he talks sounds to me like he might be charged with sody water." Gosh, I got to laffin' so I had to git right out of the cort house.

It sort of made me think of a law soot we had down hum when Jim Lawson wuz Jestice of the Peece. You see it wuz like this: One spring Si Pettingill wuz goin' out to Mizoori to be gone 'bout a year, and he'd sold off 'bout all his things 'cept one cow, and he didn't want to part with the cow, 'cause she wuz a mighty good milker, so he struck a bargin with Lige Willet. Lige wuz to keep the cow, paster and feed her, and generally take keer on her fer the milk she giv. Wall, finally Si cum hum, and he went to Lige's place one day and sed: "Wall, Lige, I've cum over to git my cow." And Lige sed: "Cum after your cow? Wall, if you've got any cow round here I'll be durned if I know it." Si sed: "Wall, Lige, I left my cow with you." And Lige sed: "Wall, that's a year ago, and she's et her head off two or three times since then." So Si sed: "Wall, Lige, you've had her milk fer her keep." And Lige sed: "Milk be durned, she went dry three weeks after you left, and she ain't give any milk since, and near as I can figger it out, seems to me as how I've pestered her and fed her all this time, she's my cow." Si sed: "No, Lige, that wa'nt the bargin." But Lige sed: "Bargin or no bargin, I've got her, and seein' as how posession is 'bout nine points in the law, I'm goin' to keep her."

So they went to law about it, and all Punkin Centre turned out to heer the trial. Wall, after Jim Lawson had heered both sides of the case, he sed: "The Cort is compelled, from the evidence sot forth in this case, to find for the plaintiff, the aforesaid Silas Pettingill, as agin' the defendant, the aforesaid Elijah Willet. We find from the evidence sot forth that the cow critter in question is a valuable critter, and wuth more 'n a year's paster and keep, and, tharfore, it is the verdict of this cort that the aforesaid defendant, Elijah Willet, shall keep the cow two weeks longer, and then she is hisn."

Uncle Josh at Coney Island

I'D heerd tell a whole lot at various times 'bout that place what they call Coney Iland, and while I wuz down In New York, I jist made up my mind I wuz a goin' to see it, so one day I got on one of them keers what goes across the Brooklyn bridge, and I started out for Coney Iland. Settin' right along side of me in the keer wuz an old lady, and she seemed sort of figity 'bout somethin' or other, and finaly she sed to me "mister, do these cars stop when we git on the other side of the bridge?" I sed, wall now if they don't you'll git the durndest bump you ever got in your life.

Wall we got on the other side, and I got on one of them tra-la-lu cars what goes down to Coney Iland. I give the car feller a dollar, and he put it in his pockit jist the same as if it belonged to him. Wall, when I wuz gittin' purty near thar I sed, Mister, don't I git any change? He sed, "didn't you see that sign on the car?" I sed, no sir. Wall he sez "you better go out and look at it."

Wall I went out and looked at it, and that settled it. It sed "This car goes to Coney Iland without change." Guess it did; I'll be durned if I got any.

Wall we got down thar, and I must say of all the pandemonium and hubbub I ever heered in my life, Coney Iland beats it all. Bout the fust thing I seen thar wuz a place what they called "Shoot the Shoots." It looked like a big hoss troff stood on end, one end in a duck pond and tother end up in the air, and they would haul a boat up to the top and all git in and then cum scootin' down the hoss troff into the pond. Wall I alowed that ud be right smart fun, so I got into one of the boats along with a lot of other folks I never seed afore and don't keer if I never see agin. They yanked us up to the top of that troff and then turned us loose, and I jist felt as though the whole earth had run off and left us. We went down that troff lickety split, and a woman what wuz settin' alongside of me, got skeered and grabbed me round the neck; and I sed, you let go of me you brazen female critter. But she jist hung on and hollered to beat thunder, and everybody wuz a yellin' all to onct, and that durned boat wuz a goin' faster'n greased lightnin' and I had one hand on my pockit book and tother on my hat, and we went kerslap dab into that duck pond, and the durned boat upsot and we went into the water, and that durned female critter hung onto me and hollered "save me, I'm jist a drownin'." Wall the water wasn't very deep and I jist started to wade out when along cum another boat and run over us, and under we went ker-souse. Wall I managed to get out to the bank, and that female woman sed I was a base vilian to not rescue a lady from a watery grave. And I jist told her if she had kept her mouth shet she wouldn't hav swallered so much of the pond.

Wall they had one place what they called the Middle Way Plesumps, and another place what they called The Streets of Caro, and they had a lot of shows a goin' on along thar. Wall I went into one of 'em and sot down, and I guess if they hadn't of shet up the show I'd a bin sottin' thar yet. I purty near busted my buttins a laffin'. They had a lot of gals a dancin' some kind of a dance; I don't know what they called it, but it sooted me fust rate. When I got home, the more I thought about it the more I made up my mind I'd learn that dance. Wall I went out in the corn field whar none of the neighbors could see me, and I'll be durned if I didn't knock down about four akers of corn, but I never got that dance right. I wuz the talk of the whole community; mother didn't speak to me fer about a week, and Aunt Nancy Smith sed I wuz a burnin' shame and a disgrace to the village, but I notice Nancy has asked me a good many questions about jist how it was, and I wouldn't wonder if we didn't find Nancy out in the cornfield one of these days.

Uncle Josh at the Opera

WALL, I sed to mother when I left hum, now mother, when I git down to
New York City I'm goin' to see a regular first-class theater. We never
had many theater doin's down our way. Wall, thar wuz a theater troop
cum to Punkin Centre along last summer, but we couldn't let 'em hav the
Opery House to show in 'cause it wuz summer time and the Opery House
wuz
full of hay, and we couldn't let 'em hav it 'cause we hadn't any place
to put the hay. An then about a year and a half ago thar wuz a troop cum
along that wuz somethin' about Uncle Tom's home; they left a good many
of their things behind 'em when they went away. Ezra Hoskins he got one
of the mules, and he tried to hitch it up one day; Doctor says he thinks
Ezra will be around in about six weeks. I traded one of the dogs to
Ruben Hendricks fer a shot gun; Rube cum over t'other day, borrowed the
gun and shot the dog.

Wall, I got into one of your theaters here, got sot down and wuz lookin'
at it; and it wuz a mighty fine lookin' pictur with a lot of lights
shinin' on it, and I wuz enjoyin' it fust rate, when a lot of fellers
cum out with horns and fiddles, and they all started in to fiddlin' and
tootin', end all to once they pulled the theatre up, and thar wuz a lot
of folks having a regular family quarrel. I knowed that wasn't any of
my business, and I sort of felt uneasy like; but none of the rest of
the folks seemed to mind it any, so I calculated I'd see how it cum out,
though my hands sort of itched to get hold of one feller, 'cause I could
see if he would jest go 'way and tend to his own business thar wouldn't

be any quarrel. Wall, jest then a young feller handed me a piece of
paper what told all about the theater doin's, and I got to lookin' at
that and I noticed on it whar it sed thar wuz five years took place
'tween the fust part and the second part. I knowed durned well I
wouldn't have time to wait and see the second part, so I got up and went
out. Wall, them theater doin's jest put me in mind of somethin' what
happened down hum on the last day of school. You see the school teacher
got all the big boys and the big girls, and the boys they read essays
and the girls recited poetry. One of the Skinner girls recited a piece
that sooted me fust rate. Neer as I kin remember it went somethin' like
this:

> How nice to hear the bumble-bee
>   When you go out a fishin',
> But if you happen to sot down on him,
>   He'll spoil your disposition.

I liked that; thar wuz somethin' so touchin' about it. Then the school
teacher he got all the girls in the 'stronomy class and he dressed
them up to represent the different kinds of planits. He had one girl to
represent the sun--she wuz red-headed; and another one to represent the
moon, and another one fer Mars, and another one fer Jerupetir, and it
looked mighty fine, and everythin' wuz a gettin' along fust rate 'til
old Jim Lawson 'lowed he could make an improvement on it; so he went out
and got a colord girl, and he wanted to sot her between the sun and the
moon and make an eklips. And as usual he busted up the whole doin's.

Uncle Josh at Delmonico's

I USED to hear the summer boarders tell a whole lot about a place here in New York kept by Mr. Delmonico. Thar's bin about ten thousand summer boarders down to Punkin Centre one time and another, and I guess I've carried the bundles and stood the grumblin' from about all of them; and when anyone of 'em would find fault with anythin' I used to ast him whar he boarded at in New York, and they all told me at Mr. Delmonico's; so I'd cum to the conclusion that Mr. Delmonico must hav a right smart purty good sized tavern; and I sed to mother--now mother, when I git down to New York that's whar I'm goin' to board, at Mr. Delmonico's.

Wall, I got a feller to show me whar it wuz, and when I got on the inside I don't s'pose I wuz ever more sot back in all my life; guess you could have knocked my eyes off with a club; they stuck out like bumps on a log. Wall sir, they had flowers and birds everywhere, and trees a settin' in wash tubs, didn't look to me as though they would stand much of a gale; and about a hundred and fifty patent wind mills runnin' all to onct, and out in the woods somewhar they had a band a-playin'. I couldn't see 'em but I could hear 'em; guess some of 'em wuz a havin' a dance to settle down their dinner; I couldn't tell whether it was a society festival or a camp meetin' at feedin' time. Wall, one feller cum up to me and commenced talkin' some furrin language I didn't understand, somethin' about bon-sour, mon-sour. I jist made up my mind he wuz one of them bunco fellers, and I wouldn't talk to him. Then another feller cum up right smart like and wanted to know if I'd hav my dinner table de hotel or all over a card, and I told him if it wuz all the same to him he could bring me my dinner on a plate. Wall, he handed me a programme of the dinner and I et about half way down it and drank a bottle of cider pop what he give me, and it got into my head, and I never felt so durn good in all my life. I got to singin' and I danced Old Dan Tucker right thar in the dinin' room, and I took a wrestle out of Mr. bon-sour mon-sour; and jist when I got to enjoyin' myself right good, they called in a lot of constables, and it cost me sixteen dollars and forty-five cents, and then they took me out ridin' in a little blue wagon with a bell on it, and they kept ringin' the bell every foot of the way to let folks know I wuz one of Mr. Delmonico's boarders.

It is Fall

THE days are gettin' shorter, and
the summer birds are leaving,

The wind sighs in the tree tops,
as though all nature was grieving;

The leaves they drop in showers, there's a
blue haze over all,

And a feller is reminded that once again it's
Fall.

It is a glorious season, the crops most gathered
in,

The wheat is in the granary and the oats are
in the bin;

A feller jest feels splendid, right in harmony
with all,

The old cider mill a-humin', 'gosh, I know
it's Fall.

I hear the Bob White whistlin' down by the
water mill,

While dressed in gorgeous colors is each
valley, knoll and hill;

The cows they are a-lowing, as they slowly
wander home,

And the hives are just a-bustin' with the
honey in the comb.

Soon be time for huskin' parties, or an apple
paring bee,

And the signs of peace and plenty are just
splendid for to see;

The flowers they are drooping, soon there
won't be none at all,

Old Jack Frost has nipped them, and by that
I know it's Fall.

The muskrat has built himself a house down
by the old mill pond,

The squirrels are laying up their store from
the chestnut trees beyond;

While walking through the orchard I can
hear the ripe fruit fall;

There's an air of quiet comfort that only
comes with Fall.

The wind is cool and bracing, and it makes
you feel first-rate,

And there's work to keep you going from
early until late;

So you feel like giving praises unto Him
who doeth all,

Nature heaps her blessings on you at this
season, and it's Fall.

The nights are getting frosty and the fire
feels pretty good,

I like to see the flames creep up among the
burning wood;

Away across the hilltops I can hear the hoot
owl call,

He is looking for his supper, I guess he
knows its Fall.

And though the year is getting old and the
trees will soon be bare,

There's a satisfactory feeling of enough and
some to spare;

For there's still some poor and needy who
for our help do call,

So we'll share with them our blessings and
be thankful that it's Fall.

Si Pettingill's Brooms

WALL, one day jist shortly after sap season wuz over, we wuz all sottin'
round Ezra Hoskins's store, talkin' on things in general, when up drove
Si Pettingill with a load of brooms. Wall, we all took a long breath,
and got ready to see some as tall bargainin' as wuz ever done in Punkin
Centre. 'Cause Si, he could see a bargain through a six-inch plank on
a dark night, and Ezra could hear a dollar bill rattle in a bag of
feathers a mile off, and we all felt mighty sartin suthin' wuz a goin'
to happen. Wall, Si, he sort er stood 'round, didn't say much, and Ezra
got most uncommonly busy--he had more business than a town marshal on
circus day.

Wall, after he had sold Aunt Nancy Smith three yards of caliker, and
Ruben Hendricks a jack-knife, and swapped Jim Lawson a plug of tobacker
fer a muskrat hide, he sed: "How's things over your way, Si?" Si
remarked: "things wuz 'bout as usual, only the water had bin most
uncommon high, White Fork had busted loose and overflowed everything,
Sprosby's mill wuz washed out, and Lige Willits's paster wuz all under
water, which made it purty hard on the cows, and Lige had to strain the
milk two or three times to git the minnews out of it. Whitaker's young
'uns wuz all havin' measles to onct, and thar wuz a revival goin' on
at the Red Top Baptist church, and most every one had got religion, and
things wuz a runnin' 'long 'bout as usual."

Deacon Witherspoon sed: "Did you git religion, Si?" Si sed: "No, Deacon;
I got baptized, but it didn't take--calculated I might as well have it

done while thar wuz plenty of water."

"Thought I'd cum over today, Ezra; I've got some brooms I'd like to sell ye." Ezra sed: "Bring 'em in, Si, spring house cleanin' is comin' on and I'll most likely need right smart of brooms, so jist bring 'em in." Si sed: "Wall, Ezra, don't see as thar's any need to crowd the mourners, can't we dicker on it a little bit; I want cash fer these brooms, Ezra, I don't want any store trade fer 'em." Ezra sed: "Wall, I don't know 'bout that, Si; seems to me that's a gray hoss of another color, I always gin ye store trade fer your eggs, don't I?" Si sed: "Y-a-s--, and that's a gray hoss of another color; ye never seen a hen lay brooms, did ye? Brooms is sort of article of commerce, Ezra, and I want cash fer 'em." Wall, Ezra, he looked 'round the store and thot fer a spell, and then he sed: "Tell ye what I'll do, Si; I'll gin ye half cash and the other half trade, how'll that be?" Si sed: "Guess that'll be all right, Ezra. Whar will I put the brooms?" Ezra sed: "Put them in the back end of the store, Si, and stack 'em up good; I hadn't got much room, and I've got a lot of things comin' in from Boston and New York." Wall, after Si had the brooms all in, he sed: "Wall, thar they be, five dozen on 'em." Ezra sed: "Sure thar's five dozen?" Si sed: "Yas; counted 'em on the wagon, counted 'em off agin, and counted 'em when I made 'em." So Ezra sed: "Wall, here's your money; now what do you want in trade?" Si looked 'round fer a spell and sed: "I don't know, Ezra; don't see anything any of our folks pertickerly stand in need on. If it's all the same to you, Ezra, I'll take BROOMS?"

Wall, Jim Lawson fell off'n a wash-tub and Ruben Hendricks cut his thumb with his new jack-knife, and Deacon Witherspoon sed: "No, Si, that baptizin' didn't take." And Ezra--wall, it wan't his say.

Suspicion--Consists mainly of thinking what we would do if
we wuz in the other feller's place.
--Punkin Centre Philosophy.

Uncle Josh Plays Golf

WALL, about two weeks ago the boys sed to me, Uncle we'd like to hav you cum out and play a game of golf. Wall, they took me out behind the woodshed whar mother couldn't see us and them durned boys dressed your uncle up in the dogondest suit of clothes I ever had on in my life. I had on a pair of socks that had more different colors in 'em than in Joseph's coat. I looked like a cross atween a monkey and a cirkus rider, and a-goin' across the medder our turkey gobbler took after me and I had an awful time with that fool bird. I calculate as how I'll git even with him 'bout Thanksgiving time.

Wall, the boys took me into the paster, and they had it all dug up into what they called a "T," and they had a wheelbarrer full of little Injun war clubs. They called one a nibbler, and another a brassie, and a lot of other fool names I never heerd afore, and can't remember now. Then they brought out a little wooden ball 'bout as big as a hen's egg, and they stuck it up on a little hunk of mud. Then they told me to take one of them thar war clubs and stand alongside of the ball and hit it. Wall, I jist peeled off my coat and got a good holt on that war club and I jist whaled away at that durned little ball, and by gum I missed it, and the boys all commenced to holler "foozle."

Wall, I got a little bit riled and I whaled away at it again, and I hit it right whar I missed it the fust time, and I whirled round and sot down so durned hard I sot four back teeth to akin, and I pawed round in the air and knocked a lot of it out of place. I hit myself on the shin and on the pet corn at the same time, and them durned boys wuz jist a-rollin' round on the ground and a-hollerin' like Injuns. Wall, I begun to git madder 'n a wet hen, and I 'lowed I'd knock that durned little ball way over into the next county. So I rolled up my sleeves and spit on my hands and got a good holt on that war club and I whaled away at that little ball agin, and by chowder I hit it. I knocked it clar over into Deacon Witherspoon's paster, and hit his old muley cow, and she got skeered and run away, jumped the fence and went down the road, and the durned fool never stopped a-runnin' 'til she went slap dab into Ezra Hoskins' grocery store, upsot four gallons of apple butter into a keg of soft soap, and sot one foot into a tub of mackral, and t'other foot into a box of winder glass, and knocked over Jim Lawson who wuz sottin' on a cracker barrel, and broke his durned old wooden leg, and then she went right out through the winder and skeered Si Pettingill's hosses that wuz a standin' thar, and they run away and smashed his wagon into kindlin' wood' and Silas has sued me fer damages, and mother won't speak to me, and Jim he wants me to buy him a new wooden leg, and the neighbors all say as how I ought to be put away some place fer safe keepin', and Aunt Nancy Smith got so excited she lost her glass eye and didn't find it for three or four days, and when she did git it the boys wuz a-playin' marbles with it and it wuz all full of gaps, and Jim Lawson he trimmed it up on the grindstane and it don't fit Nancy any more, and she has to sort of put it in with cotton round it to bold it, and the cotton works out at the corners and skeers the children and every time I see Nancy that durned eye seems to look at me sort of reproachful like, and all I know about playin' golf is, the feller what knocks the ball so durned far you can't find it or whar it does the most damage, wins the game.

Jim Lawson's Hogs

WHEN it cum to raisin' hogs, I don't s'pose thar wuz ever enybody in Punkin Centre that had quite so much trouble as Jim Lawson. One fall Jim had a right likely bunch of shoats, but somehow or other he couldn't git 'em fat, it jist seemed like the more he fed 'em the poorer they got, and Jim he wuz jist about worried clar down to a shadder. He kept givin' them hogs medecin' and feedin' of 'em everything he could think on, but it wan't no use; every day or so one of 'em would lay down and die. All the neighbors would cum and lean over the fence, and talk to Jim, and give him advice, but somehow them hogs jist kept on a-dyin', and nobody could see what wuz alin' of 'em, 'til one day Jim cum over to Ezra Hoskins's store, and he looked as tickled as though he'd found a dollar, and he sed: "I want you all to cum over to my place; I've found out what's alin' them hogs." Deacon Witherspoon sed: "Wall, what is it, Jim?" and Jim sed: "Wall, you see the ground over in my hog lot is purty soft, and when it rains it gits right smart muddy, and the mud gits on them hogs' tails, and that mud it gits more mud, and finally they git so much mud on their tails that it draws their skin so tight that they can't shet their eyes, and them hogs air jist a-dyin' fer the want of sleep."

Wall, the followin' winter Jim had his hogs all fat and ready fer markit, and he jist conclooded he'd drive 'em to Concord. Wall, he started out, and when he'd drov 'em two whole days he met old Jabez Whitaker. Jabe sed: "Whar you goin' with your hogs, Jim?" Jim sed: "Goin' to Concord, Jabez." Jabez sed "Wall, now, I want to know. That's what cums from not readin' the papers. Why, Jim, they've got more hogs up Concord way than they know what to do with. Lige Willit took his hogs up thar, and Eben Sprosby took his'n, and Concord's jist chuck full of hogs, and so consequintly the markit's away down in Concord. But the paper sez it's good in Manchester, and you'd make money, Jim, by goin' thar." So Jim shifted his chew of terbacker over to the northeast, and sed: "Wall, boys, I calculate we'll hav to go to Manchester, so jist head the hogs off and turn them round." Wall, they druv them hogs 'bout three days towards Manchester, and jist 'bout when they wuz gittin' thar, along cum Caleb Skinner, and he sed: "Wall, thunder and fish-hooks, whar be you a-goin', Jim." And Jim sed: "As near as he could figure it out from his present bearin's, he wuz most likely goin' to Manchester." And Caleb sed: "What fer?" Jim sed: "Didn't know exactly what all he wuz goin' fer, but if he ever got thar, he'd most likely sell his hogs." And Caleb sed: "Wall, your goin' to the wrong town. Manchester has got a quarantine agin' any more hogs comin' in, 'cos what hogs they is thar has all got colery, and you'd better go to Concord. Besides the paper says markit is purty well up in Concord." Wall, Jim sed a good many things that wouldn't sound good at a prayer meetin', and then he sed: "Wall, boys, gess we'll start back fer Concord, so turn round." Wall, they went along 'bout two days, and them poor hogs couldn't stand it no longer 'cos they wuz jist clean tuckered out, so Jim had to sell 'em to Josiah Martin fer what he could git, 'cos it wuz jist right at Josiah's place whar the hogs gin out, and thar wan't no way of moovin' them from thar fer some time to cum.

Wall, along 'bout two weeks after that we wuz all over to Ezra Hoskins's store, and some one sed: "Jim, you didn't do very well with your hogs this year, did you?" And Jim sed: "Oh, I don't know; that's jist owin' to how you look at it. I never caught up to that blamed markit, but I had the society of the hogs fer two weeks."

Uncle Josh and the Lightning Rod Agent

WALL I s'pose I git buncode offener than any feller what ever lived in Punkin Centre. A short time ago we wanted to build a new town hall, and calculated we'd have a brick building; and some one sed, "Wall now, if you'll jist wait 'til Josh Weathersby makes another trip or two down to New York thar'll be gold bricks enuff a-layin' 'round Punkin Centre to build a new town hall."

Wall, one day last summer I wuz a sottin' out on my back porch, when along cum one of them thar lightning rod agents. Wall, he jist cum right up and commenced a-talkin' at me jist as if he'd bin the town marshal or a tax assessor, or like he'd known me all his life. He sed, "My dear sir, I am astonished at you. I've looked over your entire premises and I find you haven't got a lightning rod on any buildin' that you possess. Why, my dear sir, don't you know you are flyin' right in the face of Providence? Don't you know that lightning may strike at any time and demolish everything within the sound of my voice? Don't you know you are criminally negligent? Why, my dear sir, I am astonished to think that a man of your jedgment and good common sense should allow yourself to----" Wall, about that time I'd got my breath and wits at the same time, and I sed, "Now hold on, gosh durn ye, what hav ye got to sell anyhow?" Wall, he told me he had some lightnin' rods, and he brought out a little masheen and told me to take hold of the handles and he'd show me what a powerful thing 'lectricity wuz. Wall, I took hold of them handles and he turned on a crank, and that durned masheen jist made me dance all over the porch, and it wouldn't let go. Gee whiz, I felt as though I'd fell in a yeller jacket's nest, and about four thousand of 'em wuz a stingin' me all to onct. Wall, I told him I guessed he could put up a lightning rod or two, seein' as how I didn't hav any. Wall, he went to work and I went over to Ezra Hoskins', and when I got back home my place wuz a sight to behold; it looked like a harrer turned upside down. Thar wuz seven lightning rods on the barn, one on the hen house, one on the corn crib, one on the smoke house, two on the granery, three on the kitchen, six on my house, and one on the crab apple tree, and when I got thar that durned fool had the old muley cow cornered up a-tryin' to put a lightnin' rod on her. Wall, I paid him fer what he had done, and thanked the Lord he hadn't done any more. Wall, he got me to sine a paper what sed he had done a good job, and he sed he had to show that to the company.

Wall, about a week after that we had a thunder storm, and I think the lightnin' struck everything on the place except the spring wagon and old muley cow, and they didn't have any lightnin' rod on 'em. Wall I thought I wuz a-gittin' off mighty lucky til next day, when along cum a feller with that paper what I had sined, and durned if it wan't a note fer six hundred dollars, and by gosh if I didn't hav to pay it!

Buncode agin, by chowder!

Energy--There is a lot of energy in this life that wasted. I notis that the man who has a good strong pipe most usually rides in front.--Punkin Centre Philosophy.

A Meeting of the Annanias Club

WALL, sometimes a lot of us old codgers used to git down to Ezra
Hoskins' grossery store and we'd sot 'round and chaw terbacker and
whittle sticks and eat crackers and cheese and proons and anything Ezra
happened to have layin' 'round loos, and then we'd git to spinnin' yarns
that would jist about put Annanias and Safiry right out of business
if they wuz here now. Wall, one afternoon we wuz all settin' 'round
spinnin' yarns when Deacon Witherspoon sed that eckos wuz mighty
peculiar things, cos down whar he wuz born and raised thar wuz a passell
of hills cum together and you couldn't git out thar and talk louder 'n
a whisper on account of the ecko. But one day a summer boarder what wuz
thar remarked as how he wasn't afraid to talk right out in meetin' in
front of any old lot of hills what wuz ever created; so he went out and
hollered jist as loud as he could holler, and he started a ecko a-goin'
and it flew up agin one hill and bounced off onto another one and
gittin' bigger and louder all the time 'til it got back whar it started
from and hit a stone quarry and knocked off a piece of stone and hit
that feller in the head, and he didn't cum too fer over three hours.
Wall, we thought that wuz purty good fer a Deacon. Wall, none of us sed
anything fer a right smart spell and then Si Pettingill remarked "he
didn't know anything about eckos, but he calculated he'd seen some
mighty peculiar things; sed he guessed he'd seen it rain 'bout as hard
as anybody ever seen it rain." Someone sed, "Wall, Si, how hard did you
ever see it rain?" and he sed, "Wall one day last summer down our way it
got to rainin' and it rained so hard that the drops jist rubbed together
comin' down, which made them so allfired hot that they turned into

steam; why, it rained so gosh dinged hard, thar wuz a cider bar'l layin'
out in the yard that had both heads out'n it and the bung hole up; wall,
it rained so hard into that bung hole that the water couldn't run out of
both ends of the bar'l fast enough, and it swelled up and busted." Wall,
we all took a fresh chew of terbacker and nudged each other; and Ezra
Hoskins sed he didn't remember as how he'd ever seen it rain quite so
hard as that, but he'd seen some mighty dry weather; he sed one time
when he wuz out in Kansas it got so tarnation dry that fish a-swimmin'
up the river left a cloud of dust behind them. And hot, too; why, it got
so allfired hot that one day he tied his mule to a pen of popcorn out
behind the barn, and it got so hot that the corn got to poppin' and
flyin' 'round that old mule's ears and he thought it wuz snow and laid
down and froze to death. Wall, about that time old Jim Lawson commenced
to show signs of uneasiness, and someone sed, "What is it, Jim?" and
Jim remarked, as he shifted his terbacker and cut a sliver off from his
wooden leg, "I wuz a-thinkin' about a cold spell we had one winter
when we wuz a-livin' down Nantucket way. It wuz hog killin' time, if I
remember right; anyhow, we had a kittle of bilin' water sottin' on the
fire, and we sot it out doors to cool off a little, and that water froze
so durned quick that the ice wuz hot."

Ezra sed, "Guess its 'bout shettin' up time."

Jim Lawson's Hoss Trade

SPEAKIN' of hoss tradin', now Jim Lawson was calculated to be about the best hoss trader in Punkin Centre. Yes, Jim he could sot up on a fence, chew terbacker, whittle a stick, and jist about swap ye outen your eye-teeth, if you'd listen to him.

Yas, Jim wuz some punkins on a swap; Jim 'd swap anything he had fer anything he didn't want, jist to be swappin'.

Wall, a gypsy cum along one day and tackled Jim fer a swap; and about that time Jim he'd got hold of a critter that had more cussedness in him to the squar inch than any critter we'd ever sot eyes on, 'cept a cirkus mule that Ezra Hoskins owned.

Wall, the gypsy traded Jim a mighty fine lookin' critter, and we all calculated that Jim had right smart of a bargain, 'til one day Jim went to ride him, 'n he found out if he fetched the peskey critter on the sides he'd squat right down. Wall, Jim knowed if he didn't git rid of that hoss, his reputation as a hoss trader wuz forever gone; so he went over in t'other township to see old Deacon Witherspoon. You see the Deacon he wuz mighty fond of goin' a-huntin', and as he had rheumatiz purty bad it wuz sort of hard fer him to git 'round, so he had to do his huntin' on hoss back. Wall, Jim didn't say much to fuss, just kinder hinted around that huntin' was a-goin' to be mighty good this fall, cos he'd seen one or two flocks of partridges over back of Sprosby's medder, and some right smart of quail over by Buttermilk ford, and finally he sed: "Deacon, I've got a hoss you ought to hev; he's a setter." Wall, you could hav knocked the Deacon's eyes off with a club, they stuck out like bumps on a log, and he sed, "Why, Jim, I never heered tell of sech a thing in all my life; the idea of a horse being a setter!" Jim sed, "Yes, Deacon, he's bin trained to set for all kinds of game. I calculated as how I'd git a shotgun this fall and do right smart of hunting." So the Deacon sed, "Wall, now, I want to know; bring him over, Jim, I'd like to see him."

Wall, Jim took the hoss over, and all Punkin Centre jest sort of held its breath to see how it would cum out.

Jim and the Deacon went a-hunting, and as they wuz a-ridin' along through the timber down by Ruben Hendrick's paster, Jim keepin' his eyes peeled and not sayin' much, when all to onct he seen a rabbit settin' in a brush heap, and he jist tetched the old hoss on the sides and he squatted right down. The Deacon sed, "Why, what's the matter of your hoss, Jim, look what he be a doin'." Jim sed, "'Sh, Deacon, don't you see that rabbit over thar in the brush heap? the old hoss is a-settin' of him." Deacon sed, "Wall, now that's the most remarkable thing I ever seen in my life; how'd you like to trade, Jim?" Jim sed, "Wall, Deacon, I hadn't calculated on disposin' of the hoss, but I ain't much of a hand at huntin', and seein' as how it's you, if you want him I'll trade you, Deacon, fifty dollars to boot."

Wall, the Deacon had a mighty fine animal, but he sed, "I'll trade you, Jim." They traded hosses, and when they wuz a-comin' home they had to ford the crick what runs back of Punkin Centre, and when the old hoss wuz a-wadin' through the water, Deacon went to pull his feet up to keep them from gettin' wet, and he tetched the old boss on the sides and he squatted right down in the crick. Deacon sed, "Now look a-here, Jim, what's the matter with this ungodly brute, he ain't a-settin' now be he?" Jim sed, "Yes he is, Deacon, he sees fish in the water; tell you he's trained to set fer suckers same as fer rabbits, Deacon; oh, he's had a thorough eddication."

Paradox--I can't exactly describe it, but it looks to me
like a tramp who once told me how to be successful in life.
--Punkin Centre Philosophy.

A Meeting of the School Directors

WE had bin havin' a good deal of argufyin' about the school house. You see it had got to be a sort of a tumble-down ram-shackle sort of an affair, and when it wuz bad weather we couldn't have school in it, 'cause you might jist as well be a sittin' under a siv when it rained as to be a settin' in that school house. Wall, it wuz a-cummin' along the fall term, and we wanted our boys and girls to git all the schoolin' an' eddication what they could; so we called a meetin' of the school directors to devise ways and means of buildin' a new school-house without stoppin' school. Wall, we all met down at the school-house; thar wuz Deacon Witherspoon, Ezra Hoskins, Ruben Hendricks, Si Pettingill, old Jim Lawson and me. Before we commenced debatin' and argufyin' on the matter, Si Pettingill alowed he'd sing a song. Wall, he got up and sang the durndest old-fashioned song I calculate I ever heered in my life; went somethin' like this:

> Oh a frog went a courtin' and he did ride,
>
>   oohoo--oohoo.
>
> Oh a frog went a courtin' and he did ride,
>
> With a sword and a pistol by his side,
>
>   oohoo--oohoo.
>
> He rode till he came to the mouse's door,
>
>   oohoo--oohoo,
>
> He rode till he came to the mouse's door,
>
> And there he knelt upon the floor,
>
>   oohoo--oohoo.

He took Miss Mousey on his knee,
>   oohoo--oohoo.
He took Miss Mousey on his knee,
Said he, Missy Mouse will you marry me?
>   oohoo--oohoo.

Wall, we headed Si off right thar; I guess if we hadn't he'd bin singin' about that frog and the mouse yet. Wall, jist then old Jim Lawson he sed, "I make a moshen;" and Deacon Witherspoon, he wuz chairman, and he sed, "Now look here, young feller, don't you make any moshens at me or durned if I don't git down thar and flop you in about a minnit. You take your feet off'n that desk and that corncob pipe out'n your mouth, and conduct yourself with dignity and decorum, and address the chairman of this yere meetin' in a manner benttin' to his station." Wall, Jim he got right smart riled over the matter, and he sed, "Wall, you gosh durned old gospel pirate, I want you to understand that I'm a member of this body, a citizen, a taxpayer and a honorably discharged servant of the government, and I make a moshen that we build a new school-house out of the bricks of the old school-house, and I do further offer an amendment to the original moshen, that we don't tear down the old schoolhouse until the new one is built."

Wall, Deacon Witherspoon sed, "The gentleman is out of order;" and Jim sed, "I ain't so durned much out of order but that I kin trim you in about two shakes of a dead sheep's tail." Wall, before we knowed it, them two old cusses wuz at it. The Deacon he grabbed Jim and Jim he grabbed the Deacon, and when we got 'em separated the Deacon he wuz stuck fast 'tween a desk and the woodbox, and Jim had his wooden leg through a knot hole in the floor and couldn't get it out, and they've both gone to law about it. Jim says he's goin' to git out a writ of corpus cristy fer the Deacon, and the Deacon says he's goin' to prosecute Jim for bigamy and arson and have him read out of the church.

Wall, we've got the same old schoolhouse.

Justice--Those who hanker fer it would be generally better off if they didn't git it.--Punkin Centre Philosophy.

The Weekly Paper at Punkin Centre

WALL, t'other day, down in New York, I wuz a-walkin' along on that
street what they call the broad way, when I cum to the Herald squar
noospaper buildin', and it wuz all winders and masheenery. Wall, I wuz
jist flobgasted; I jist stood thar lookin' at it. On the front thar
wuz a bell and a couple of fellers standin' along side of it with slege
hammers in their hands, and every onct in a while they would go to
poundin' on that bell, and folks 'd stand 'round and watch 'em do it;
they reminded me of a couple of fellers splittin' rales. And all 'round
the edge of the buildin' they had hoot owls sottin', with electric lites
in their ize, and thar wuz no end to the masheenery in that buildin'. If
anyone hed ever told me thar wuz that much masheenery in the whole world
durned if I'd a-beleeved them; biggest masheen I'd ever seen before
wuz Si Pettingill's new thrashin' masheen. Wall, I jist stood thar
a-watchin' them printin' presses a-runnin'; paper goin' in to one end
and cumin' out at t'other all printed and full of picters and folded up
ready to sell; it jist beat all the way they done it. Wall, we never
had but one paper down home at Punkin Centre; we called it "The Punkin
Centre Weakly Bugle;" old Jim Lawson he wuz editor of it. You see Jim
he wuz sort of a triflin' no 'count old cuss, so to keep him out of
mischief we made him editor. Wall, Jim he had his place up over
Ezra Hoskins' grossery store. He never got any money for the
noospaper--always got paid in produce, and Ezra's store wuz a mighty
good place fer him to take in his subskriptions. Wall, things went along
pretty smooth fer quite a spell 'til one day a feller he cum in and give
Jim a keg of hard cider fer a year's subskription to the noospaper, and

we all calculated right then that somethin' wuz a-goin' to happen; and sure enough it did. You see 'bout that time Jim had got two advertisements; one wuz fer Ruben Jackson's resterant and the other wuz the time table of the Punkin Centre and Paw Paw Valley Railroad. Wall, Jim he got to drinkin' the hard cider and settin' type at the same time, and when the paper cum out on Thursday it wuz wuth goin' miles to see. Neer as I kin remember it sed that: "Ruben Jackson's resterant would leave the depo every mornin' at eight o'clock fer beefstake and mutton stews, and would change cars at White River Junkshen for mins and punkin pise, and cottage puddin' would be a flag stashen fer coffy and do nuts like mother used to make, and the train wouldn't run on Sundays cos the stashun agint what done the cookin' would have to run en extra on that day over the chicken and ham sandwitch divishion."

I believe that wuz the last issu of the Punkin Centre Weakly Bugle.

Enthusiasm--Sometimes inspired, sometimes acquired, sometimes the result of immediate surroundings, and sometimes the result of hard cider.--Punkin Centre Philosophy.

Uncle Josh at a Camp Meeting

WALL, we've jist bin havin' a camp meeting at Punkin Centre. Yes, fer several days we wuz purty busy bakin' and cookin and makin' preparations fer the camp meetin', and some of the committee alowed we ought to have lemonade fer the Sunday school children. Wall, as we wanted to git it jist as cheap as possible, we damed up the crick what runs back of the camp meeting grounds, and put in ten pounds of brown sugar and half a dozen lemons, and let the Sunday school children drink right out of the crick, free of charge. Wall, we had right smart difficulty in gittin' a pulpit fixed up fer the ministers, but finally we sawed down a hemlock tree and used the stump fer a pulpit. Wall, some of the sarmons preached at that camp meetin' beat anything I ever heered in my life afore. You see we'd bin havin' a good many argyments 'bout corporations, monopolies and trusts, and one minister got up and sed, "Ah, my dear beloved brethren and sisters, we should not be too severe on the monopolists. If we read the scripters closely we observe our forefathers wuz all monopolists. Adam and Eve had a monopoly upon the garden of Eden, and would have had it 'til this day, no doubt, had not Mother Eve got squeezed in the apple market. Yea, verily, Lot's wife had a corner on the salt market. And while Pharoe's daughter was not in the milk business, yet we observe she took a great proffit out of the water; yea, verrily." Most on us cum to the conclusion he wuz ridin' on a free pass.

Samantha Hoskins concluded she would have to sing her favorit hymn; it went something like this:

"Oh you need not cum in the mornin',
   And neither in the heat of the day;
But cum along in the evenin', Lord,
   And wash my sins away.

Chorus--
Standin' on the walls of Zion,
   Lookin' at my ship cum a sailln' ov{er};
Standin' on the walls of Zion,
   To see my ship cum in."

Jist about that time Ruben Hendricks skeered a skunk out of a holler
log. Si Pettingill stirred up a hornet's nest, Deacon Witherspoon sot
down in a huckleberry pie and Aunt Nancy Smith got a spider on her, and
she started in to yellin' and jumpin' like she had a fit, and two dogs
got to fitin', and old Jim Lawson he tried to git 'em apart and he
stumped 'round and got his old wooden leg into a post hole and fell
down, and the dogs got on top of him, and you couldn't tell which wuz
Jim nor which wuz dog; and durned if it didn't bust up the camp meetin'.

The Unveiling of the Organ

IT wuz down in Punkin Centre,
   I believe in eighty-nine,
We had some doin's at the meetin' house,
   That we thought wuz purty fine;

It wuz a great occasion,
   The choir, led by Sister Morgan,
Had called us thar to witness
   The unveilin' of the organ.

In order fer to git it
   We'd bin savin' here and there,
Lookin' forward to the time
   When we'd have music fer to spare,
And as the time it had arrived,
   And the organ had cum, too,
We had all of us assembled thar
   To hear what the thing could do.

Wall, it wuz a gorgeous instrument,
   In a handsome walnut case,
And thar wuz expectation
   Pictured out on every face;
Then when Deacon Witherspoon
   Had led us all in prayer,

The congregation all stood up
  And Old Hundred rent the air.

Jist then the doin's took a turn,
  Though I'm ashamed to say it,
We found that old Jim Lawson
  Wuz the only one could play it;
But Jim, the poor old feller,
  Had one besettin' sin,
A fondness fer hard cider
  Which he'd bin indulgin' in.

But he sot down at that organ,
  Planked his feet upon the pedals,
And he showed us he could play it
  Though he hadn't any medals;
He dwelt upon the treble
  And he flirted with the base,
He almost made that organ
  Jump right out of its case.

Wall, the cider got in old Jim's head
  And in his fingers, too,
So he played some dancin' music
  And old Yankee Doodle Doo;
He shocked old Deacon Witherspoon
  And scared poor Sister Morgan,
And jist busted up the meetin'
  At the unveilin' of the organ.

Uncle Josh Plays a Game of Base Ball

I HAD heered a whole lot 'bout them games of foot ball they have in New York, so while I was thar I jist cum to the conclusion I'd see a game of it, so went out to one of their city pasters to see a game of foot ball. Wall now I must say I didn't see much ball playin' of any kind. All I got to see wuz about fifty or sixty ambulances, and I think about that many surgons and phisicians. Wall, from what I could see of the game I calculate they needed all of them. I saw one feller and 'bout fifty others had him down, and it jist looked as though they wuz all trying to get a kick at him. They had a half back and a quarter back; I suppose when they got through with that feller he wuz a hump back. Anyhow, if that's what they call foot ball playin', your Uncle Josh don't want any foot ball in his'n.

I never played but one game of ball in my life that I kin remember on, and don't believe that I ever will forget that. You see it wuz along in the spring time of the yeer, and the weather wuz purty warm and sunshiny, and the boys sed to me, "Uncle, we'd like to have you help us play a game of base ball." I sed, "Boys, I'm gittin' a little too old fer those kinds of passtimes, but I'll help you play one game, I'll be durned if I don't." Wall, we got out in the paster and wuz gittin' ready to play; we got the bases and bats put around in thar places, and a buckit of drinkin' water up in the fence corner, whar we could get a drink when we wanted it. We didn't have any bleachers, but we had thirty or forty hogs, and they wuz the best rooters you ever seen; jist then I happened to look around and thar wuz the biggest billy goat I ever saw

in all my life. You ought to seen the boys a-gittin' out of the paster;
I would hav got out too, but I got stuck in the fence. Wall, you ought
to hav seen that billy goat a-gittin' me through the fence. He didn't
git me all the way through, cos I wuz half way through when he got thar;
but he got the last half through. I didn't make any home run, but I wuz
the only feller what had a score of the game; I couldn't see the score,
but I had it. Every time I'd go to sot down I knowed jist exactly how
the game stood.

They hav a good many new fangled games now, but when they git anything
that can beet a game of base ball with a billy goat fer a battery,
durned if I don't want to see it.

The Punkin Centre and Paw Paw Valley Railroad

WONDERS will never cease--we've got a railroad in Punkin Centre now; oh, we're gittin' to be right smart cityfied. I guess that's about the crookedest railroad that ever wuz bilt. I think that railroad runs across itself in one or two places; it runs past one station three times. It's so durned crooked they hav to burn crooked wood in the ingine. Wall, the fust ingine they had on the Punkin Centre wuz a wonderful piece of masheenery. It had a five-foot boiler and a seven-foot whissel, and every time they blowed the whissel the durned old ingine would stop.

Wall, we've got the railroad, and we're mighty proud of it; but we had an awful time a-gittin' it through. You see, most everybody give the right of way 'cept Ezra Hoskins, and he didn't like to see it go through his medder field, and it seemed as though they'd hav to go 'round fer quite a ways, and maybe they wouldn't cum to Punkin Centre at all. Wall, one mornin' Ezra saw a lot of fellers down in the medder most uncommonly busy like; so he went down to them and he sed, "Wat be you a-doin' down here?" And they sed, "Wall, Mr. Hoskins, we're surveyin' fer the railroad." And Ezra sed, "So we're goin' to hav a railroad, be we? Is it goin' right through here?" And they sed, "Yes, Mr. Hoskins, that's whar it's a-goin', right through here." Ezra sed, "Wall, I s'pose you'll have a right smart of ploughin' and diggin', and you'll jist about plow up my medder field, won't ye?" They sed, "Yes, Mr. Hoskins, we'll hav to do some gradin'." Ezra sed, "Wall, now, let me see, is it a-goin' jist the way you've got that instrument p'inted?" They sed, "Yes, sir, jist thar." And Ezra sed, "Wall, near as I kin calculate from that, I should jedge it wuz a-goin' right through my barn." They sed, "Yes, Mr. Hoskins, we're sorry, but the railroad is a-goin' right through your barn."

Wall, Ezra didn't say much fer quite a spell, and we all expected thar would be trouble; but finally he sed, "Wall, I s'pose the community of Punkin Centre needs a railroad and I hadn't oughter offer any objections to its goin' through, but I'm goin' to tell ye one thing right now, afore you go any further. When you git it bilt and a-runnin', you've got to git a man to cum down here and take keer on it, cos it's a-cumin' along hayin' and harvestin' time, and I'll be too durned busy to run down here and open and shet them barn doors every time one of your pesky old trains wants to go through."

Love--An indescribable longing, something that existed since Mother Eve was in the apple trust, and will exist until the end of time. Somethin' that no man has ever yet defined or ever will define. A somethin' that is past all description. Which will make a hired man fergit to do the chores, and will make an old man act boyish, and will make a woman show herself to be stronger than the strongest man. Gosh durn it, an indescribable somethin' that has never yet bin described.
--Punkin Centre Philosophy.

Uncle Josh on a Bicycle

A LONG last summer Ruben Hoskins, that is Ezra Hoskins' boy, he cum home from college and bro't one of them new fangled bisickle masheens hum with him, and I think ever since that time the whole town of Punkin Centre has got the bisickle fever. Old Deacon Witherspoon he's bin a-ridin' a bisickle to Sunday school, and Jim Lawson he couldn't ride one of them 'cause he's got a wooden leg; but he jist calculated if he could git it hitched up to the mowin' masheen, he could cut more hay with it than any man in Punkin Centre. Somebody sed Si Pettingill wuz tryin' to pick apples with a bisickle.

Wall, all our boys and girls are ridin' bisickles now, and nothin' would do but I must learn how to ride one of them. Wall, I didn't think very favorably on it, but in order to keep peace in the family I told them I would learn. Wall, gee whilikee, by gum. I wish you had bin thar when I commenced. I took that masheen by the horns and I led it out into the middle of the road, and I got on it sort of unconcerned like, and then I got off sort of unconcerned like. Wall, I sot down a minnit to think it over, and then the trouble commenced. I got on that durned masheen and it jumped up in the front and kicked up behind, and bucked up in the middle, and shied and balked and jumped sideways, and carried on worse 'n a couple of steers the fust time they're yoked. Wall, I managed to hang on fer a spell, and then I went up in the air and cum down all over that bisickle. I fell on top of it and under it and on both sides of it; I fell in front of the front wheel and behind the hind wheel at the same time. Durned if I know how I done it but I did. I run my foot through the spokes, and put about a hundred and fifty punctures in a hedge fence, and skeered a hoss and buggy clar off the highway. I done more different kinds of tumblin' than any cirkus performer I ever seen in my life, and I made more revolutions in a fifteen-foot circle than any buzz-saw that ever wuz invented. Wall, I lost the lamp, I lost the clamp, I lost my patience, I lost my temper, I lost my self-respect, my last suspender button and my standin' in the community. I broke the handle bars, I broke the sprockets, I broke the ten commandments, I broke my New Year's pledge and the law agin loud and abusive language, and Jim Lawson got so excited he run his wooden leg through a knot-hole in the porch and couldn't git it out agin. Wall, I'm through with it; once is enough fer me. You kin all ride your durned old bisickles that want to, but fer my part I'd jist as soon stand up and walk as to sit down and walk. No more bisickles fer your Uncle Josh, not if he knows it, and your Uncle Josh sort of calculates as how he do.

Notoriety--A next door neighbor to glory, but another way of gittin' it.--Punkin Centre Philosophy.

A Baptizin' at the Hickory Corners Church

A LONG about two summers ago we had a baptizin' at the Hickory Corners Church, and before the baptizin' we had preachin', and before the preachin' we had Sunday school. Wall now, some of them questions and answers in that Sunday school jist made me snicker right out loud. You see, old Deacon Witherspoon wuz a-teachin' the Sunday school class, and he sed, "Now let me see what little boy can tell me who slew the Philistines and whar at?" Wall, no one sed anything fer about a minnit, then a little red-headed feller down at the foot of the class sed, "Commodore Dewey, at Manila." The Deacon sed, "No, Henry, it wasn't Commodore Dewey what slew the Philistines, it wuz Sampson." Another little feller sed, "No, Deacon, I think you've sort of got it mixed up; he wasn't there; Schley is the feller what done the job, at Santiague." The Deacon sed, "Now, boys, you've bin readin' too much about them war doin's in the papers. Now what little boy can tell me what is the first commandment?" And Ezra Hoskins' boy sed, "Remember the main." Gosh, I had to go right out of the meetin' house, whar I could have a good laugh. Wall, I wouldn't have bin down thar in the fust place, or the second place, fer that matter, if it hadn't bin fer old Jim Lawson. You see, Jim he's a peculiar old critter. He's got one eye out; lost it lookin' fer a pension, I believe. Wall, Jim he cum over to my house and he sed, "Josh, let's you and me go down to the baptizin'." I sed, "What do you want to go down thar fer, Jim; you can't git any pension thar, kin ye?" Jim sed, "Wall, you see, Josh, thar wuz a pedler left some hymn books at my house, and I want to go down thar and see if I can't sell 'em." Wall, we hadn't bin thar more 'n a minnit when Jim he told the minister he had the hymn books to sell, and the minister sed he'd tell the congregation all about it. Then Jim he sot right down in the meetin' house and went to sleep; and then he went to snorin'; you could hear him clar across a forty acre lot. I wouldn't a-keered a gosh durn, but he woke me up Wall, about the time the minister wuz a-gittin' through with his sermon, he sed, "Now all members of the congregation having babies here to-day and wantin' of them baptized after the sermon is over, bring them up to the pulpit and I will baptize them." Wall, Jim he woke up about that time, and he thought the minister wuz a-talkin' about his hymn books; so he stood up and sed, "Now all you folks what ain't got any I'll let ye have 'em, twenty-five cents apiece."

Religion--Any one man's opinion, but consists mainly of doing right.--Punkin Centre Philosophy.

Reminiscence of My Railroad Days

Dedicated to Engineer John Hoolihan, Pittsburg and Lake Erie Railroad,
Pittsburg, Pa.

WALL, John, I read your poetry,
   And laughed till I nearly cried,
Seein' how you became an engineer,
   And got on the right hand side.
It made me think of the days gone by,
   When I wuz one of you fellers, too,
What used to run an old machine,
   And go tootin' the country through.
But the engine that I had then, John,
   Wuz far from a "Nancy Hanks;"
She wuz old and worn and loggy,
   And jist chuck full of pranks;
And she wuz wonderfully got up, John,
   Full of bolts and valves and knobs,
And the boiler wouldn't hold water;
   Gosh, it wouldn't hold cobs.

But I wuz younger then, John,
   And I didn't care a cuss;
So I'd pull the throttle open
   And jist let her wheeze and fuss.
The road that I wuz a-runnin' on

Wuz out in the woolly west;
Two streaks of rust and the right of way
   Wuz puttin' it at its best.
So we sort of plugged along, John.
   And didn't put on any frills,
Never thought of doin' anything
   But doublin' all the hills.
I tell you those were rocky times,
   And we hadn't no air brake;
And fifteen miles an hour, John,
   Wuz durn good time to make.

And thar wuz as good a lot of boys
   As you could meet with anywhere;
Rough and ready open up,
   And always on the square.
And I'd like to see them all again,
   And grasp each honest hand;
But some of them, like me, have quit,
   Some have gone to another land.
I have changed somewhat since then, John,
   Jist a little more steady grown;
But I often think of my railroad days
   As the happiest ones I've known.
And, John, I often watch the train.
   As they go whizzing by;
As I think of Bill, or Jim, or Jack,
   Thar's a tear comes in my eye.

Perhaps you'd like to know, John,
   Just why I quit the rail,
And as some feller one time sed,
   "Thereby hangs a tale."

I wuz goin' along one night, John,
   At a purty lively rate,
The old machine a-doin' her best,
   And me forty minutes late,
When all at once there came a crash,
   I felt the old track yield,
And fireman, machine and I
   Went into a farmer's field.
There's little more to say, John,
   They laid me up for repairs,
But my fireman, poor fellow,
   Hadn't time to say his prayers.

So now you have my story, John;
   Still, you don't know how it feels
To know you've got to plug around
   On a couple of flat wheels.
But it doesn't bother me, John,
   Gosh, not fer a minnit;
I'm as happy as the day is long,
   And feel jist strictly in it.
But sometimes I like to meet the boys,
   And talk them days all over,
And I feel as gay and chipper
   As a calf in a field of clover
But the happiest days I've known, John,
   The ones that to me see best,
Wuz when I run an old machine
   Way out in the woolly west.

Glory--Gittin' killed and not gittin' paid fer it.
--Punkin Centre Philosophy.

Uncle Josh at a Circus

WALL, 'long last year, 'bout harvest time, thar wuz a cirkus cum to Punkin Centre, and I think the whole population turned out to see it. They cum paradin' into town, the bands a-playin' and banners flying, and animals pokin' their heads out of the cages, and all sorts of jim cracks. Deacon Witherspoon sed they wuz a sinful lot of men and wimmin, and no one aughter go and see them, but seein' as how they wuz thar, he alowed he'd take the children and let them see the lions and tigers and things. Si Pettingill remarked, "Guess the Deacon won't put blinders on himself when he gits thar." We noticed afterwards that the Deacon had a front seat whar he could see and hear purty well.

Wall, I sed to Ezra Hoskins, "Let's you and me go down to the cirkus," and Ezra sed, "All right, Joshua." So we got on our store clothes, our new boots, and put some money in our pockits, and went down to the cirkus. Wall, I never seen any one in my life cut up more fool capers than Ezra did. We got in whar the animals wuz, and Ezra he walked around the elefant three or four times, and then he sed, "By gum, Josh, that's a durned handy critter--he's got two tails, and he's eatin' with one and keepin' the flies off with t'other." Durned old fool! Wall, we went on a little ways further, and all to onct Ezra he sed, "Geewhiz, Josh, thar's Steve Jenkins over thar in one of them cages." I sed, "Cum along you silly fool, that ain't Steve Jenkins." Ezra sed, "Wall, now, guess I'd oughter know Steve Jenkins when I see him; I jist about purty near raised Steve." Wall, we went over to the cage, and it wan't no man at all, nuthin' only a durned old baboon; and Ezra wanted to shake hands with him jist 'cause he looked like Steve. Ezra sed he'd bet a peck of pippins that baboon belonged to Steve's family a long ways back.

Wall then we went into whar they wuz havin' the cirkus doin's, and I guess us two old codgers jist about busted our buttins a-laffin at that silly old clown. Wall, he cut up a lot of didos, then he went out and sot down right alongside of Aunt Nancy Smith; and Nancy she'd like to had histeericks. She sed, "You go 'way from me you painted critter," and that clown he jist up and yelled to beat thunder--sed Nancy stuck a pin in him. Wall, everybody laffed, and Nancy she jist sot and giggled right out. Wall, they brought a trick mule into the ring, and the ring master sed he'd give any one five dollars what could ride the mule; and Ruben Hoskins alowed he could ride anything with four legs what had hair on. So he got into the ring, and that mule he took after Ruben and chased him 'round that ring so fast Ruben could see himself goin' 'round t'other side of the ring. He wuz mighty glad to git out of thar. Then a gal cum out on hoss back and commenced ridin' around. Nancy Smith sed she wuz a brazen critter to cum out thar without clothes enough on her to dust a fiddle. But Deacon Witherspoon sed that wuz the art of 'questrinism; we all alowed it, whatever he meant. And then that silly old clown he told the ring master that his uncle committed sooiside different than any man what ever committed sooiside; and the ring master sed, "Wall, sir, how did your uncle commit sooiside?" and that silly old clown sed, "Why, he put his nose in his ear and blowed his head off." Then he sang an old-fashioned song I hadn't heered in a long time; went something like this:

From Widdletown to Waddletown is fifteen miles,
   From Waddletown to Widdletown is fifteen miles,
From Widdletown to Waddletown, from Waddletown
      to Widdletown,
Take it all together and its fifteen miles.

He wuz about the silliest cuss I ever seen. Wall, I noticed a feller a rummagin' 'round among the benches as though he might a-lost somethin'. So I sed to him, "Mister, did you lose anythin' 'round here any place?" He sed, "Yes, sir, I lost a ten dollar bill; if you find it I'll give you two dollars." Wall, I jist made up my mind he wuz one of them cirkus sharpers, and when he wan't a-lookin' I pulled a ten dollar bill out of my pockit and give it to him; and the durned fool didn't know but what it wuz the same one that he lost. Gosh, I jist fooled him out of his two dollars slicker 'n a whistle. I tell you cirkus day is a great time in Punkin Centre.

Uncle Josh Invites the City Folks to Visit Him

I DIDN'T s'pose when I wuz gittin' ready to go home, that all you folks would be down here to the depo' to see me off. Wall, now, that's purty good of ye, I'll be durned it it ain't. Yes, I guess I'll have to be goin' home now; I've stayed here this time 'bout as long as I kin afford to. I must say, some of you folks have made it purty warm fer me since I've bin here in New York; but I guess I've enjoyed it 'bout as much as you have.

I'd like to have you all cum down to Punkin Centre and see MEE some time this summer, if you hadn't got nuthin' else to do. Lots of fun down thar on that farm of mine, huntin', fishin', and shootin', and other things. Wall, I never shot but one bird in my life, and that wuz a squirrel; yes, sir, a flyin' squirrel.

I had a feller workin' fer me on the farm last summer, and he was cross-eyed, and I sent him out in the paster to dig a well fer me, and what do you s'pose? Wall he dug it so tarnal all-fired crooked that he fell out of it and sprained his ankel. Then one day I sent him out in the garden to plant some pertaters and some unyuns fer me, and it jist seemed like that feller didn't have good hoss sense. He planted them unyuns and pertaters right alongside of each other, and the unyuns got into the pertaters' eyes and they couldn't see to grow. Oh, yes, lots of fun down home onct in a while. I calculate I've got the funnyest lot of chickens you ever heerd tell on. I've got sixty old hens and they lay an egg every day; but they don't lay any at nite, cos when nite comes every

one of them is roosters. I had one old hen, she went into the woodshed
and sot down on the ax and tried to hatch-it. I had another one sottin'
on a door knob, tryin' to hatch out a house and lot, but she didn't.
While she wuz a-sottin' there along cum a rooster, and he sed, "We're
having a little party down behind the barn; will you dance with me this
set?" and she sed, "No, sir, I'm engaged to his nobs for this set."
Gosh, I wuz afraid to go out in the barnyard one while, cos one day
when I wuz out thar I heerd a hen say to a rooster, "Thar's that old
gray-headed cuss we've bin a-layin' fer."

Guess that's my train; s'pose I'll have to be a-goin'; good-bye; cum
down and see me some time if you kin, ev'ry one of ye; cum down about
apple-butter time and jist butt in--good bye.

Yosemite Jim, or a Tale of the Great White Death

YOSEMITE JIM wuz the name he had,
    And he came from no one knowed whar;
Quiet, easy goin' sort of a cuss,
    And wuz reckoned on the squar'.
Ridin' a route for the Wells Fargo folks
    May have made him stern and grim;
But thar wasn't a man that crossed the divide
    But 'ud swar by Yosemite Jim.

He wa'n't one of the regular sort
    What you'd meet thar any day,
But as near as the camp could figure it out,
    In a show down he'd likely stay.
A shambling, awkward figure,
    Rawboned, tall and slim,
And his schaps and togs in general
    Jist looked like they'd fell on him.

I wuz somewhat of a tenderfoot then,
    Hadn't jist got the lay of the land;
Thar wuz a good many things in them thar parts
    As I couldn't quite understand.
But I took a likin' to Yosemite Jim,
    Wuz with him on my very first trick;

And from that time on I stuck to him
　　Like a kitten to a good warm brick.

Our headquarters then wuz the valley camp,
　　It wuz down by the redwood way,
　With Chaparel across the spur,
　　'Bout fifty miles away.
Wall, what I'm goin' to tell you, pard,
　　Happened thar whar the trail runs into the sky;
And if it hadn't a-bin fer Yosemite Jim,
　　Wall, I'd be countin' my chips on high.

The galoot that wuz punchin' the broncos fer me
　　Wuz a greaser from down Monterey;
And Jim used to say, "Keep your eye on him, pard,
　　I don't think he's cum fer to stay;
His eyes are too shifty and yeller,
　　And his face is sullen and hard;
And 'taint that so much as a feelin' I have;
　　Anyhow, keep your eye on him, pard."

One day when the mercury wuz way out of sight,
　　And the frost it wuz on every nail,
With jist the mail sack and specie box,
　　The greaser and I hit the trail.
We picked two passengers up at Big Pine,
　　And while the broncos were changed that day
I noticed them havin' a sneakin' chat
　　With the greaser from down Monterey.

Did you ever hear tell of the Great White Death,
　　That creeps down the mountain side,
Leavin' behind it a ghastly track

Whar those who have met it died?
Wall, pard, as true as I'm a-livin',
    No man wants to see it twice;
White and grim as a funeral shroud,
    A mass of mist and ice.

Wall, we hadn't got far from the Big Pine relay
    When my hair it commenced to rise,
For I saw across by the Lone Bear spur
    A cloud of most monstrous size.
And the greaser acted sort of peculiar,
    And the broncos commenced to neigh;
Wall, some thoughts went through my mind jist then
    I won't forgit till my dyin' day.

In less time than it takes to tell it,
    We were into the Great White Death,
With its millions of frozen snowflakes
    A-takin' away our breath.
And jist then somethin' happened, pard,
    The greaser from down Monterey
Tried to sneak off with the specie box,
    Along with the passengers from Big Pine relay.

All at once a figure on hossback
    Cum a-whoopin' it down the trail,
And bullets from out of a Winchester
    Commenced to fly like hail.
The greaser and them two passengers
    Cashed in their chips to him,
Fer the feller what wuz doin' the shootin'
    Wuz my friend, Yosemite Jim.

Wall, we planted them thar together,
  When the cloud had passed away;
And all they've got fer a tombstone
  Is the mountains, dull and gray.
So, pard, let's take one together,
  And I'll drink a toast to him,
Fer though he wuz rough and ready,
  He'd a heart, YOSEMITE JIM.

The Great White Death, so named by the Indians, occurs in the higher altitudes of the Rocky and Sierra Nevada Mountains. It is almost indescribable. It might properly be termed a frozen fog. It has the effect of bringing on acute congestion of the lungs, from which few rarely recover. Viewed at a distance it is a magnificent sight, each and every particle of the frozen moisture being a miniature prism, which reflects the sun's rays in a manner once seen never to be forgotten.--By CAL. STEWART, formerly Overland Messenger for the Wells-Fargo Express Company.

Uncle Josh Weathersby's Trip to Boston

FER a long time I had my mind made up to go down to Boston, so a short time ago, as I had all my crops and produce mostly sold, I alowed it would be a good time to go down thar, and I sed to mother, "I'll start early in the mornin' and take a load of produce with me, and that will sort of pay expenses of the trip."

Wall, I got into Boston next mornin' bright and early, 'bout time they had their breakfast, and I looked 'round fer a spell; then finally I picked out a right likely lookin' store, and jist conclooded I'd sell my load of produce thar. Wall, I went in and I met a feller 'nd I sed, "Good mornin', be you the storekeeper?" And he sed, "No, sir, I'm only one of the clerks." So I sed, "Wall, be the storekeeper to hum?" And he sed, "Yes, sir, would you like to see him?" And I told him as how I would, and he turned 'round and commenced to hollerin' "FRONT," and a boy cum up what had more brass buttins on him than a whole regiment of soljers. I thought that wuz a durned funny name fer a boy--front--and that clerk feller he wuz about the most importent thing I'd seen in Boston so far, less maybe it wuz the Bunker Hill monument that I druv past cummin' to town. He had on a biled collar that sort of put me in mind of the whitewashed fence 'round the fair grounds down hum. I'll bet if he'd ever sneeze it would cut his ears off.

Wall, anyhow, he sed to that front boy, "Show the gentleman to the proprietor's offis." Wall, I went along with that boy, and presently we cum to a place in one corner of that store; it wuz made out of iron and had bars in front of the winders, and looked like the county jale. The front boy p'inted to a man and sed, "Go in," and I sed, "I gessed I wouldn't go in thar, cos I hadn't done anything to be locked up fer." And that front boy commenced to laffin' tho' durned if I could see what he wuz a-laffin' about, and the storekeeper he opened the door and cum out, and he sed, "Good mornin', what can I do fer you?" I sed, "Be you the storekeeper?" and he sed he wuz. So I sed, "Do you want to buy any pertaters?" And he sed, "No, sir, we don't buy pertaters here; this a dry goods store." So I sed, "Wall, don't want any cabbage, do ye?" And he sed, "No, sir, this is a dry goods store." So I sed, "Wall, now, I want to know; do you need any onions?" And by chowder, he got madder 'n a wet hen. He sed, "Now look a-heer, I want you to understand onct fer all, this is a dry goods store, and we don't buy anything but dry goods and don't sell anything but dry goods; do you understand me now? DRY GOODS." And I sed, "Yes, gess I understand you; you don't need to git so tarnaly riled about the matter; neer as I can figure it out you jist buy dry goods and sell 'em." And he sed, "Yes, sir, only dry goods." So I sed, "Do you want to buy some mighty good dried apples?"

Wall, that front boy got to laffin, and a lot of wimmin clerks giggled right out, and the storekeeper he commenced a-laffin', too, and fer about a minnit I thought they'd all went crazy to onct. Wall, he told a feller to show me whar I could sell my produce, and I disposed of it at a good bargain.

I like them Boston folks, they try to make you feel to hum, and enjoy yourself and be soshable, and I wuz chuck full of soshability, too; I wuz goin' up one street and down t'other, jist a-gettin' soshability at ten cents a soshable.

Wall, I gess I seen about everything wuth seein' in Boston, and I wuz a-standin' along-side of one of their old churches, a-lookin' at the semetry, and I gess thar wuz folks in thar burried nigh unto three hundred years. And I wuz jist a-thinkin' what they'd say if they could wake up and see Boston now, when I noticed a row of little toomstones, and one of them it sed, "Hester Brown, beloved wife of James Brown," and on another it sed, "Prudence Brown, beloved wife of James Brown," and on another it sed, "Thankful Brown, beloved wife of James Brown." Wall, I couldn't jist make out what she had to be thankful about, but I sed, "Jimmy, you had a right lively time while you wuz in Boston, didn't you?" Then I seen another toomstone and on it it sed, "Matilda Brown, beloved wife of James Brown," and another one what sed,

"Sara Ann Brown, beloved wife of James Brown," and over in a little corner, all to itself, I seen a toomstone, and on it it sed, "James Brown, At Rest."

Who Marched in Sixty-One

CAL STEWART, New York, Memorial Day, 1903.

I'VE jist bin down at the corner, mother,
    To see the boys in line,
Dressed up in their bran' new uniforms,
    I tell you they looked fine.
And as they marched past whar I stood,
    To the rattle of the drum,
It made me think of those other boys
    Who marched in sixty-one.

The old flag wuz proudly wavin', mother,
    Jist as it did one day
When you stood thar to say good-bye,
    And watch me march away.
So I stood thar and watched them
    Till the parade wuz nearly done,
But thar wasn't many thar to-day
    Who marched in sixty-one.

And thar wuz my old Captain
    And the Colonel side by side,
And as they both saluted me
    I jist sot down and cried.

And I thought about some other boys
   Whose work has long bin done;
Soon thar won't be any left at all
   Who marched in sixty one.

I heered the band play Dixie,
   And my old heart swelled with pride,
A-thinkin' of the boys in gray
   Who marched on the other side.
And when my time it comes, mother,
   The Lord's will it be done,
I hope he'll take me to the boys
   Who marched in sixty-one.

The Codes Of Hammurabi And Moses
W. W. Davies

QTY

The discovery of the Hammurabi Code is one of the greatest achievements of archaeology, and is of paramount interest, not only to the student of the Bible, but also to all those interested in ancient history...

Religion   ISBN: *1-59462-338-4*

Pages:132
MSRP $12.95

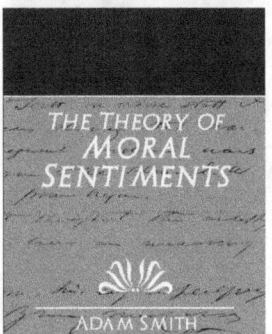

The Theory of Moral Sentiments
Adam Smith

QTY

This work from 1749. contains original theories of conscience amd moral judgment and it is the foundation for systemof morals.

Philosophy ISBN: *1-59462-777-0*

Pages:536
MSRP $19.95

Jessica's First Prayer
Hesba Stretton

QTY

In a screened and secluded corner of one of the many railway-bridges which span the streets of London there could be seen a few years ago, from five o'clock every morning until half past eight, a tidily set-out coffee-stall, consisting of a trestle and board, upon which stood two large tin cans, with a small fire of charcoal burning under each so as to keep the coffee boiling during the early hours of the morning when the work-people were thronging into the city on their way to their daily toil...

Childrens   ISBN: *1-59462-373-2*

Pages:84
MSRP $9.95

My Life and Work
Henry Ford

QTY

Henry Ford revolutionized the world with his implementation of mass production for the Model T automobile. Gain valuable business insight into his life and work with his own auto-biography... "We have only started on our development of our country we have not as yet, with all our talk of wonderful progress, done more than scratch the surface. The progress has been wonderful enough but..."

Biographies/   ISBN: *1-59462-198-5*

Pages:300
MSRP $21.95

The Art of Cross-Examination
Francis Wellman

QTY

I presume it is the experience of every author, after his first book is published upon an important subject, to be almost overwhelmed with a wealth of ideas and illustrations which could readily have been included in his book, and which to his own mind, at least, seem to make a second edition inevitable. Such certainly was the case with me; and when the first edition had reached its sixth impression in five months, I rejoiced to learn that it seemed to my publishers that the book had met with a sufficiently favorable reception to justify a second and considerably enlarged edition. ..

Pages:412

Reference   ISBN: *1-59462-647-2*   *MSRP $19.95*

On the Duty of Civil Disobedience
Henry David Thoreau

QTY

Thoreau wrote his famous essay, On the Duty of Civil Disobedience, as a protest against an unjust but popular war and the immoral but popular institution of slave-owning. He did more than write—he declined to pay his taxes, and was hauled off to gaol in consequence. Who can say how much this refusal of his hastened the end of the war and of slavery ?

Law   ISBN: *1-59462-747-9*   **Pages:48**

MSRP $7.45

Dream Psychology Psychoanalysis for Beginners
Sigmund Freud

QTY

Sigmund Freud, born Sigismund Schlomo Freud (May 6, 1856 - September 23, 1939), was a Jewish-Austrian neurologist and psychiatrist who co-founded the psychoanalytic school of psychology. Freud is best known for his theories of the unconscious mind, especially involving the mechanism of repression; his redefinition of sexual desire as mobile and directed towards a wide variety of objects; and his therapeutic techniques, especially his understanding of transference in the therapeutic relationship and the presumed value of dreams as sources of insight into unconscious desires.

Pages:196

Psychology   ISBN: *1-59462-905-6*   *MSRP $15.45*

The Miracle of Right Thought
Orison Swett Marden

QTY

Believe with all of your heart that you will do what you were made to do. When the mind has once formed the habit of holding cheerful, happy, prosperous pictures, it will not be easy to form the opposite habit. It does not matter how improbable or how far away this realization may see, or how dark the prospects may be, if we visualize them as best we can, as vividly as possible, hold tenaciously to them and vigorously struggle to attain them, they will gradually become actualized, realized in the life. But a desire, a longing without endeavor, a yearning abandoned or held indifferently will vanish without realization.

Pages:360

Self Help   ISBN: *1-59462-644-8*   *MSRP $25.45*

www.bookjungle.com *email: sales@bookjungle.com fax: 630-214-0564 mail: Book Jungle PO Box 2226 Champaign, IL 61825*

QTY

The Rosicrucian Cosmo-Conception Mystic Christianity by *Max Heindel* ISBN: *1-59462-188-8* **$38.95**
The Rosicrucian Cosmo-conception is not dogmatic, neither does it appeal to any other authority than the reason of the student. It is: not controversial, but is: sent forth in the, hope that it may help to clear.. New Age/Religion Pages 646

Abandonment To Divine Providence by *Jean-Pierre de Caussade* ISBN: *1-59462-228-0* **$25.95**
"The Rev. Jean Pierre de Caussade was one of the most remarkable spiritual writers of the Society of Jesus in France in the 18th Century. His death took place at Toulouse in 1751. His works have gone through many editions and have been republished... Inspirational/Religion Pages 400

Mental Chemistry by *Charles Haanel* ISBN: *1-59462-192-6* **$23.95**
Mental Chemistry allows the change of material conditions by combining and appropriately utilizing the power of the mind. Much like applied chemistry creates something new and unique out of careful combinations of chemicals the mastery of mental chemistry... New Age Pages 354

The Letters of Robert Browning and Elizabeth Barret Barrett 1845-1846 vol II ISBN: *1-59462-193-4* **$35.95**
by *Robert Browning* and *Elizabeth Barrett* Biographies Pages 596

Gleanings In Genesis (volume I) by *Arthur W. Pink* ISBN: *1-59462-130-6* **$27.45**
Appropriately has Genesis been termed "the seed plot of the Bible" for in it we have, in germ form, almost all of the great doctrines which are afterwards fully developed in the books of Scripture which follow... Religion/Inspirational Pages 420

The Master Key by *L. W. de Laurence* ISBN: *1-59462-001-6* **$30.95**
In no branch of human knowledge has there been a more lively increase of the spirit of research during the past few years than in the study of Psychology, Concentration and Mental Discipline. The requests for authentic lessons in Thought Control, Mental Discipline and... New Age/Business Pages 422

The Lesser Key Of Solomon Goetia by *L. W. de Laurence* ISBN: *1-59462-092-X* **$9.95**
This translation of the first book of the "Lernegton" which is now for the first time made accessible to students of Talismanic Magic was done, after careful collation and edition, from numerous Ancient Manuscripts in Hebrew, Latin, and French... New Age/Occult Pages 92

Rubaiyat Of Omar Khayyam by *Edward Fitzgerald* ISBN:*1-59462-332-5* **$13.95**
Edward Fitzgerald, whom the world has already learned, in spite of his own efforts to remain within the shadow of anonymity, to look upon as one of the rarest poets of the century, was born at Bredfield, in Suffolk, on the 31st of March, 1809. He was the third son of John Purcell.... Music Pages 172

Ancient Law by *Henry Maine* ISBN: *1-59462-128-4* **$29.95**
The chief object of the following pages is to indicate some of the earliest ideas of mankind, as they are reflected in Ancient Law, and to point out the relation of those ideas to modern thought. Religiom/History Pages 452

Far-Away Stories by *William J. Locke* ISBN: *1-59462-129-2* **$19.45**
"Good wine needs no bush, but a collection of mixed vintages does. And this book is just such a collection. Some of the stories I do not want to remain buried for ever in the museum files of dead magazine-numbers an author's not unpardonable vanity..." Fiction Pages 272

Life of David Crockett by *David Crockett* ISBN: *1-59462-250-7* **$27.45**
"Colonel David Crockett was one of the most remarkable men of the times in which he lived. Born in humble life, but gifted with a strong will, an indomitable courage, and unremitting perseverance... Biographies/New Age Pages 424

Lip-Reading by *Edward Nitchie* ISBN: *1-59462-206-X* **$25.95**
Edward B. Nitchie, founder of the New York School for the Hard of Hearing, now the Nitchie School of Lip-Reading, Inc, wrote "LIP-READING Principles and Practice". The development and perfecting of this meritorious work on lip-reading was an undertaking... How-to Pages 400

A Handbook of Suggestive Therapeutics, Applied Hypnotism, Psychic Science ISBN: *1-59462-214-0* **$24.95**
by *Henry Munro* Health/New Age/Health/Self-help Pages 376

A Doll's House: and Two Other Plays by *Henrik Ibsen* ISBN: *1-59462-112-8* **$19.95**
Henrik Ibsen created this classic when in revolutionary 1848 Rome. Introducing some striking concepts in playwriting for the realist genre, this play has been studied the world over. Fiction/Classics/Plays 308

The Light of Asia by *sir Edwin Arnold* ISBN: *1-59462-204-3* **$13.95**
In this poetic masterpiece, Edwin Arnold describes the life and teachings of Buddha. The man who was to become known as Buddha to the world was born as Prince Gautama of India but he rejected the worldly riches and abandoned the reigns of power when... Religion/History/Biographies Pages 170

The Complete Works of Guy de Maupassant by *Guy de Maupassant* ISBN: *1-59462-157-8* **$16.95**
"For days and days, nights and nights, I had dreamed of that first kiss which was to consecrate our engagement, and I knew not on what spot I should put my lips..." Fiction/Classics Pages 240

The Art of Cross-Examination by *Francis L. Wellman* ISBN: *1-59462-309-0* **$26.95**
Written by a renowned trial lawyer, Wellman imparts his experience and uses case studies to explain how to use psychology to extract desired information through questioning. How-to/Science/Reference Pages 408

Answered or Unanswered? by *Louisa Vaughan* ISBN: *1-59462-248-5* **$10.95**
Miracles of Faith in China Religion Pages 112

The Edinburgh Lectures on Mental Science (1909) by *Thomas* ISBN: *1-59462-008-3* **$11.95**
This book contains the substance of a course of lectures recently given by the writer in the Queen Street Hall, Edinburgh. Its purpose is to indicate the Natural Principles governing the relation between Mental Action and Material Conditions... New Age/Psychology Pages 148

Ayesha by *H. Rider Haggard* ISBN: *1-59462-301-5* **$24.95**
Verily and indeed it is the unexpected that happens! Probably if there was one person upon the earth from whom the Editor of this, and of a certain previous history, did not expect to hear again... Classics Pages 380

Ayala's Angel by *Anthony Trollope* ISBN: *1-59462-352-X* **$29.95**
The two girls were both pretty, but Lucy who was twenty-one who supposed to be simple and comparatively unattractive, whereas Ayala was credited, as her Bombwhat romantic name might show, with poetic charm and a taste for romance. Ayala when her father died was nineteen... Fiction Pages 484

The American Commonwealth by *James Bryce* ISBN: *1-59462-286-8* **$34.45**
An interpretation of American democratic political theory. It examines political mechanics and society from the perspective of Scotsman James Bryce Politics Pages 572

Stories of the Pilgrims by *Margaret P. Pumphrey* ISBN: *1-59462-116-0* **$17.95**
This book explores pilgrims religious oppression in England as well as their escape to Holland and eventual crossing to America on the Mayflower, and their early days in New England... History Pages 268

QTY

The Fasting Cure by *Sinclair Upton* ISBN: *1-59462-222-1* **$13.95**

In the Cosmopolitan Magazine for May, 1910, and in the Contemporary Review (London) for April, 1910, I published an article dealing with my experiences in fasting. I have written a great many magazine articles, but never one which attracted so much attention... New Age/Self Help/Health Pages 164

Hebrew Astrology by *Sepharial* ISBN: *1-59462-308-2* **$13.45**

In these days of advanced thinking it is a matter of common observation that we have left many of the old landmarks behind and that we are now pressing forward to greater heights and to a wider horizon than that which represented the mind-content of our progenitors... Astrology Pages 144

Thought Vibration or The Law of Attraction in the Thought World ISBN: *1-59462-127-6* **$12.95**

by *William Walker Atkinson* Psychology/Religion Pages 144

Optimism by *Helen Keller* ISBN: *1-59462-108-X* **$15.95**

Helen Keller was blind, deaf, and mute since 19 months old, yet famously learned how to overcome these handicaps, communicate with the world, and spread her lectures promoting optimism. An inspiring read for everyone... Biographies/Inspirational Pages 84

Sara Crewe by *Frances Burnett* ISBN: *1-59462-360-0* **$9.45**

In the first place, Miss Minchin lived in London. Her home was a large, dull, tall one, in a large, dull square, where all the houses were alike, and all the sparrows were alike, and where all the door-knockers made the same heavy sound... Childrens/Classic Pages 88

The Autobiography of Benjamin Franklin by *Benjamin Franklin* ISBN: *1-59462-135-7* **$24.95**

The Autobiography of Benjamin Franklin has probably been more extensively read than any other American historical work, and no other book of its kind has had such ups and downs of fortune. Franklin lived for many years in England, where he was agent... Biographies/History Pages 332

Name	
Email	
Telephone	
Address	
City, State ZIP	

☐ **Credit Card** ☐ **Check / Money Order**

Credit Card Number	
Expiration Date	
Signature	

Please Mail to: Book Jungle
PO Box 2226
Champaign, IL 61825
or Fax to: 630-214-0564

ORDERING INFORMATION

web*: www.bookjungle.com*
email*: sales@bookjungle.com*
fax*: 630-214-0564*
mail*: Book Jungle PO Box 2226 Champaign, IL 61825*
or PayPal *to sales@bookjungle.com*

Please contact us for bulk discounts

DIRECT-ORDER TERMS

**20% Discount if You Order
Two or More Books**
Free Domestic Shipping!
Accepted: Master Card, Visa,
Discover, American Express